EMBER

EMBER

Emerald Trilogy: Book 1

QUINN MINNICH

Illustrated by Anya Minnich

Quinn Minnich

Contents

To the Lord my God,
who guided me in my writings,
and taught me many things through this tale.
May it be used for His glory,
and may my heart always be led by my Rider.

...and to Liana,
whose encouragement helped me to finish this story.
I will always be thankful for her enthusiasm.

Prologue

I remember the days of my former master. They are distant and cold—buried by time, heartache, and pain—but I will never forget what they were like. I remember the man whom I used to serve, the one to whom I devoted everything—my guide, my master. Life was simple then, when we flew together to the farthest ends of the world; I was his dragon, and he was my Rider.

It's difficult to describe what our relationship was like. I was his servant, but I never felt servile. It wasn't servitude as is thought of now—it was as if he were a part of me and I of him. It was as if he were somehow the home of my soul and though I would roam about, I never strayed too far, and I always came back. Like an arm is to the body, so was I to my Rider. I was an extension of him, as if he moved through me. My joy was his joy, and if I pleased him then we rejoiced together, just as the body rejoices with the mind, even though it is subject to it.

You might gain the impression that I was enslaved—that I should have been miserable in my position—but never since have I experienced such joy. You might accuse me of being simpleminded and easily led, but I was never more in command of myself, and never sharper in mind, than when I was with him. You say that maybe it was love, that I was blinded by some romantic attachment; however, if it was love (and I can think of no other word to describe it) then it was nothing like the love we understand. It was as if he were all that mattered to me; my life and my joys were his and my actions mattered not except for how they impacted him. With him I did not even fear death. That isn't to say I wasn't afraid—I was just as afraid of death and pain as I am now, just as all creatures are—but it didn't *rule* me. If I was to do my master's will, then no fear or pain could deter me. If it was for him, then I feared nothing. Somehow, when enslaved to that man, I felt purely free.

The idea is so peculiar to me now. Looking back, I ponder what it was that kept me there. Certainty he did love me—in fact he loved me more than I loved him—but it was not his warm feelings for me that bound me. It might have been that I had something with him that I do not have now, that I have never found in all my wanderings. I had peace. There is no other way to describe it. I was content, I was at ease, and while there were pains and hardships, my soul was somehow always calm. It was as if I was where I belonged, as if I had found a niche that perfectly fit me. Life was simple; I loved him, and his will was mine. There was not the burden I now have, of what to do, of how to live, of whether or not what I do is right; I simply followed him. Not that he controlled my every action, but just that his *will* was mine—how I expressed or followed it was up to me. But who I was and what I was to do, my purpose and my meaning, those were never in question. I was his, and that was all that mattered.

I long for him again, though I know it can never be. To feel that peace again—to know that I am not in the wrong, to live in harmony under another's care—that I crave. You call me broken, you call me foolish and enslaved, you say that I am simpleminded to desire enslavement, but I care not what you say. The fact is we are all enslaved. It may be to masters, it may be to causes or kingdoms, it may even be to ourselves—we cannot escape being servants...but we can choose whom to be servants to. That is why I have chosen this path. I am driven to have purpose one more time, to finally come to rest where I belong. That is why I walk toward my own death. I want to feel that peace one more time, to know that if I am to die at least I died in my place. Yes, I miss the pleasure, the feelings of love and warmth, the fearlessness I once possessed, but they are not the reasons I lay down my life. I will die, but I will die where I belong. I will die finally free.

That is my choice, and this is my story.

I

The Dragon Rider

Once upon a time, there was a great land called Tarenthia. It was a land surrounded by sea, covering many thousands of miles and filled with forests, mountains, marshes, plains, and deserts. But its most diverse characteristic of all was its great variety of people, for within Tarenthia multitudes of small kingdoms and separate nations abounded. Now some of these civilizations built grand castles and others constructed tents; some were mighty peoples with large armies, others were but small family tribes; some traded with each other and formed alliances, others lived by themselves; and still others hated each other. But while all of these peoples did not always live in harmony, war never broke out for long; for while all of the nations were allowed to live as they chose, they all knew that one kingdom, greater than any, was watching over them all with the Dragon Rider keeping the peace.

This great kingdom was called Highland, for it lay to the west among the great highlands of Tarenthia by the Sea. It was by far the oldest, the strongest, and the mightiest kingdom in the entire land. Multiple layers of walls defended its common people, and within those walls were greater and higher walls for the nobles. Within those stood the greatest and the grandest castle in the entire world; it was within this castle that the King of Tarenthia lived. This King ruled over all the nations of the land, but he allowed them to live and prosper as they pleased. Only if there was war or conflict would the King set out from his castle and take whatever action was necessary to quell the rebellion and reconcile the people.

Now each of the Kings of Highland throughout the centuries had been known for their great wisdom, kindness, and fairness with which they judged the many disputes brought from kingdoms and nations. This was because each King followed an ancient tradition of training his son to take up the crown after him—a method that involved a dragon and a Dragon Rider.

Our story takes place at a time when all of Tarenthia was under the rule of a King who possessed so much wisdom and treated the people with such fairness that he was renowned as greater than all his fathers before him. Now, this King had ruled for many years; he knew that one day he would pass on the crown and that in order to do so he would need to prepare one of his sons to be just as wise and fair as he. The King had two sons—the older was called Justice and the younger was called Peace, and as they grew he watched them carefully to see which would have the makings of a great ruler. In his wisdom, he trained Justice to be a leader of his armies and fair judge in his courts; Peace, however, he chose to become the Dragon Rider.

***

Peace, at eight years of age, knelt in the center of the room and watched the green dragon egg. To his right, a fire burned in the great fireplace, and behind him stood the King along with many of the nobles. The fire burned softly, sending orange light across the room, and Peace sat down on the thick elaborate rug, feeling the tassels brush his fingers as he rubbed his hand back and forth. He watched the egg in front of him as it rocked; today was the day that he would be given his dragon.

Peace was, of course, elated. Dragons were rare, being found only high in the wild north, and those were fierce, dangerous dragons. But many, many years before, a wise king had traveled to the north and persuaded one of the dragons to return with him to Highland. That dragon laid eggs in Highland which began the new race of Rider dragons. They never hatched unless they were paired with a human, and very rarely did any human receive such an honor. The King had his own dragon, Glory, but aside from her no dragon had been born in Highland for many years...none, that is, until now.

Soon, the egg began to shudder and crack, and Peace watched with growing excitement. He had always been fascinated by dragons, devoting all the time and energy of his eight years into studying them; for knowledge of dragons was a required topic of his education as a member of the royal family. Now he would finally have one of his own.

Before long, the egg broke and out emerged a green dragon about the size of a kitten. Shakily, it stood on its feet and sniffed around as it tried to understand its new surroundings.

With all the excitement of a young child, yet with the gentleness he was known for, Peace reached forward and tenderly picked up the dragon, cradling it in his arms and stroking its scales. Carefully, he scooted his way across the rug and brought the dragon closer to the fire to keep it warm. He felt it wiggle in his arms into a secure position, and then it rubbed its nose against his chest. Peace held it all the more closely.

"What will you call him?" asked the King, for it was tradition that the Dragon Rider name his own dragon.

Peace looked into the fire and hugged the treasured thing he held in his arms. "I will call him Ember," he said. "For as an ember gives warmth to the soul, so he does to me; and as an ember grows to become a fire, so may he become."

"Well said!" declared the King. "And as you have called him, so shall he be. Behold everyone, for here before us is the next Dragon Rider pair—Peace, my son, and Ember, his dragon."

Everyone in the room cheered and applauded for the bond of love that had begun between the boy and the dragon, for the day of a dragon's birth is always seen as one of the happiest in a Rider's life.

Perhaps it is good, then, that happy moments are not tainted with the emotions of those that come later; for if the nobles could see to a future day that would come as a result of this occasion, they would've wept much harder than they had cheered. But perhaps it is the will of God that such things do not happen, for no one could predict where this day of rejoicing would lead, and so there was only happiness and joy in the hearts of the people.

**

Much can be said about the following years—indeed, a whole book could be written about them. But it is enough to note that Peace grew up alongside his dragon and loved him more and more each day. The dragon, of course, grew quickly until he was the size of a large dog and had to be kept outside the palace.

But until then, Peace either slept with him or played with him at nearly all hours of the day. When Ember was moved outside, Peace would vigorously complete all his schooling and other tasks in order to spend more time with his pet. His brother, Justice, was a bit jealous when he saw this, for he had no dragon of his own, but he let it rest because he was a fair child and knew that if his father had seen it fit to give the dragon to Peace, then it must be best for the kingdom.

The one day worth recounting from Peace's happy childhood, was the day that he and Ember received their Links. Now a Link was an ornament made up of a small jewel-encrusted gold cross meant to be worn around the neck on a chain. They had first been created, many years before, as a means of communicating with dragons and were a special honor given only to dragons and their Riders. The Links had an enchantment upon them which allowed he who wore one to sense the thoughts and emotions of any dragon within range. Dragons could also use the Links, but the effect upon them was greatly diminished, allowing them to only hear the thoughts of any dragon or human who was part of the Rider Pact. This limitation, however, was of little consequence because the main purpose of the Links was to provide a means of communication between a Rider and his dragon over a distance. The Link Ceremony was of great importance, as it signified the beginning of the bond which defined a Dragon Rider.

The ceremony took place in the same room in which Ember had been born. There was a fire roaring in the great fireplace, casting its orange glow across the room as the King entered with a small chest—engraved with designs and encrusted with many jewels for the sake of its valuable treasure within. The King set it down and opened it, carefully removing one of the Links and handing it to Peace, for it was tradition for a Rider to place the Link on his dragon. Feeling its light weight, Peace took it by the chain and brought it to Ember who waited at the other end of the

room. He bowed his head as Peace came and allowed the boy to place the ornament around his neck.

Immediately, Ember was able to feel the emotions of another consciousness, and he looked up into the boy's eyes and felt, for the first time, the excitement his master felt.

Peace then returned to his father who gave him the other Link. Peace took it, placed it around his own neck, and for the first time felt the excitement that Ember was feeling.

Overcome, Peace ran with great joy across the room towards Ember and wrapped his arms around his neck.

I love you, Ember.

I love you too, my young Rider; you would not believe how often I have longed to talk with you! There are so many things I wanted to ask, so many things I wanted to say...

Peace listened happily with his eyes closed, basking in the joy and excitement that poured out from his dragon. Then very quietly, in a thought that was nearly too faint to understand, he whispered an expression of his strong feelings.

I love you Ember, my Eldar.

Eldar is a Tarenthian term that does not have any direct translation. It implies the idea of both a valued teacher and a beloved friend and is therefore a word of both great love and respect. It is a term used only between Riders and their dragons.

"Very good!" said the King, no doubt remembering the occasion in which he had first spoken with his own dragon. "Now you'll be able to communicate and experience each other's feelings. Please use this gift wisely, as it is given to no one else. I must remind you that each Link *receives* the thoughts of the other. If you lose yours, you will no longer be able to hear the thoughts of your comrade, although he will still know yours. And remember that if you ever must leave each other, the Links have a limited range—about a mile of distance.

"Now, may you become the greatest Dragon Rider pair that our world has ever known, and may your reign across this land prosper!"

And with that, the nobles in the room cheered, Peace hugged Ember more closely than ever before, and Ember purred with joy—for now Ember was more than just a pet, he was Peace's lifelong companion.

***

And so the years went on. Peace and Ember spent more time apart, but communicating through the Links more and more often, as they came of the age to be trained for the Sending Out. Peace studied fencing and the art of diplomacy, while Ember spent more time with Glory, the King's dragon, to learn the art of flying with a rider, and navigating from the air. All of these were skills they would need when sent out into the expanses of Tarenthia to keep the peace among the many nations and peoples.

As the boy and dragon grew, Peace became tall and handsome while Ember, even at his young age, could stand with his shoulder level with Peace's head. Together, they would fly out over the countryside when their lessons were done, and drink in the joy of freedom and their friendship. Their shadow fell upon many of the people of Highland, and soon they became known and respected by all within the great kingdom. Many

days did they fly together, and many more did they dream of the time when they would be sent into the hinterlands with only each other.

And then, finally, the momentous day of the Sending Out arrived.

The event was held in none other than the royal throne room itself. Peace and Ember stood side-by-side before the King, with all the nobles and a great crowd of citizens standing behind them. A feeling of excitement and emergence was in the air, but no one was more excited than the Dragon and Rider.

I can hardly wait until it is just you and me over the wilderness of Tarenthia, said Ember.

Indeed, said Peace through the Link. *I long for the time when we can simply fly together without anyone else bothering us.* There was silence for a moment, and then Peace added, *I hope that we can indeed help the nations, and that during our time peace will reign.*

Yes, I'm sure it will.

Peace turned to smile at Ember. *You know, it will be dangerous. People may try to kill us.*

Through the Link, he felt Ember laugh. *Anyone that wants to kill you will have to go through me first.*

Yes, they will, my Eldar. Peace looked forward again just in time to see the King rising from his throne to welcome the assembly.

"My good people, today we have gathered here for the great Sending Out of our famed Rider. After today, he will no longer be called a citizen of Highland, but rather a ranger of Tarenthia!"

At this point the crowd cheered and the King waited several moments before raising his scepter to quiet the room.

"This is an ancient tradition that we honor today, but it is also our wisest and most important. Today, my son Peace and his dragon Ember will embark on a journey throughout the land to learn of the many kingdoms, help many nations, and quell many wars. The purpose of this is three-fold.

"First, it will ensure that when my son comes home and the crown is given to him, he will know the many ways and customs of the nations that we guard. No King is truly fit for the throne until he has walked among the streets of his own people.

"The second purpose is that in working out the conflicts between the nations, both Rider and Dragon shall gain invaluable knowledge in handling affairs and in making correct decisions that will come with being king.

"And finally, the Pact of the Dragon Rider will teach both my son and his dragon how to work together and solve problems that they will no doubt see in different ways."

At this point, Peace looked over at Ember, who winked at him.

The King continued, "When they return, they will have become experienced leaders, renowned warriors, and legendary figures, loved by the people and fit to rule the people. For ten years they shall roam the wilds of Tarenthia, and when they return they will each be given a new name to reflect who they have become. Then I shall proclaim Peace "King of Highland," and Ember shall rule at his side!"

As the King finished his speech, the people in the room gave a cheer such as Peace had never heard before. He looked back at the applauding people and then toward his father standing straight and tall before the throne with the great and heavy Sword of the Kings strapped to his side.

To the right of the King stood Glory, as powerful and magnificent as ever. Ember looked up toward the great dragon, who was black as midnight and over three times his size. She and the King wore their own Links, and Ember was able to sense Glory's thoughts as easily as he could those of Peace. He felt a great love in her for the King, a quiet love, yet somehow deeper, stronger, and more fundamental than any that even Ember had ever known. It was as though Glory found all the desires of her heart met, simply by being in the King's presence. Ember turned toward the King and felt from him the same deep desire to be in Glory's presence.

Ember bowed his head. *Someday I shall learn to love like that*, he thought to himself.

As the cheering in the room began slowly to die down, Peace looked to the King's left and saw his older brother, Justice, standing there. He stood straight and serious, like a solider, for Justice was not one to show emotion even at great occasions such as this.

The only emotion Justice ever expressed was anger—and that only when dealing with criminals, for he had no tolerance for those who broke the laws of the kingdom. The King had seen this and placed Justice in charge of the courts. None could have done a finer job than he. When faced with a case, Justice was known for relentlessly seeking out the truth at all costs and punishing the guilty to the full extent of the law.

And no one was a greater fighter than Justice. Even today he carried his weapons of choice—a dagger made for blocking and throwing, and a curved sword that he had named a katana. He could throw either weapon with deadly accuracy, and it was said that he could fight off an experienced solider with only his dagger, three men at once with his sword, and five when he wielded them both. There were many nations in which Justice was a legend and very few that did not know his name.

As Peace looked up at Justice, he saw his brother look back at him and, for just a moment, smile. Peace felt a sense of relief. He had always wondered if Justice felt jealous of him for being the Rider, but he could see that Justice loved his rank as the King's personal assistant and greatest servant. There was no rivalry between them, only pride and gladness for the other's fate. The King had been wise in choosing their positions.

"And now," came the King's booming voice as the cheering began to die down completely. "Let us end this great day with the Pledges of Loyalties."

Ember nodded and stepped forward. Having known the pledge by heart, he turned to face Peace and said to him,

I pledge my loyalty, my allegiance, and my service to my Rider. May I always be led by his command, and may my actions be done first for his good and then for the good of Tarenthia.

The King nodded and Ember took a step back, still looking at Peace. Peace smiled back, for he knew that Ember meant every word. Of course, no one else in the room without a Link had heard him, but that did not matter. The pledge was meant to be heard by only one.

"And now you, my son."

Peace stepped forward and faced the King, for this was tradition.

"I pledge my loyalty, my allegiance, and my service to the throne. May I always lead my dragon to do what is right, and may my actions be done first for his good and then for the good of Tarenthia."

"Very good!" said the King. "Now as you have pledged, so may you do. Ride forth now and become the Dragon Rider!"

Once again, and for the last time that day, there arouse from the crowd a deafening cheer and this time both Peace and Ember turned to face it. Grinning with the joy of the occasion, Peace hugged Ember around the neck and then hoisted himself up onto his back.

The crowd parted before them as they proudly walked out of the great doors of the throne room, down the hall, and toward the gates. Warm sunlight spilled down on them as they stepped out into the open air and Peace took a moment to look around him at all the people cheering and waving at them. Then, with a burst of power that shook the ground, Ember leapt into the air and spread his great wings. With awe and excitement, the people watched as the dragon and his Rider mounted higher and higher into the air, and then turned and flew east toward the boundaries of Highland.

* * *

From the window of his throne room, the King watched his son disappear into the sunlight, the way he himself had left so many years ago. He sighed deeply and as he did so Justice came to his side.

"Does something trouble you father?" he asked.

The King looked at him for a moment before speaking. "I only hope that they remain safe. There are many people out there who will try to kill them."

"I wouldn't worry about that. No one has ever overwhelmed a Dragon Rider pair before."

"I know. But still, he is very young...I hope that he can manage."

"Don't worry about Peace," said Justice. "He has Ember to protect him."

The King nodded and looked back out the window toward the sun. "Yes, I know...but it isn't Peace I am worried about."

2

The Scheme

And so, Peace and Ember traveled the expanse of Tarenthia, fulfilling the duties expected of a Rider pair. For three years they explored the land, met and spoke to great kings, and kept the peace throughout the whole country. Sometimes they were asked to be messengers to other kingdoms, and sometimes they acted as mediators between kingdoms. They journeyed on, exploring ancient ruins, discovering hidden relics, and assisting kings and citizens when they needed help.

And so, for three years peace and prosperity ruled the land, and for those three years the Dragon Pair was loved and praised by most in the kingdoms. Of course, some of the rulers held grudges because they were found to have been in the wrong, and still others had never liked the kingdom of Highland in the first place. But for the most part, Peace and Ember were loved and welcomed wherever they went. Some attempts were made to take their lives, but these were usually contrived out of hate and, therefore, rash and not well planned.

But not all the plans were feeble. There was in fact one schemer, unbeknownst to the Rider and his dragon, who had been waiting a very long time for his chance to take revenge—and his moment to strike was almost upon them.

***

In a dark room at the top of a tower near the eastern sea, a group of men gathered around a table. Eight were ordinary men from various kingdoms; the ninth was their commander. Midnight moonlight poured its pale glow through the only window while a heated discussion rang through the stony room.

"I don't see why we haven't struck by now!" growled one of the men. "You promised us a kingdom! You promised we would rule Highland! Why have we not made our move?"

"Be patient," said their leader from the head of the table. Moonlight fell across his mouth, the rest of his face shadowed by darkness. "Patience is the key to making this work. Without patience my plan will come to nothing."

"But we have waited three years!" cried the first man.

"Yes!" complained another. "We should've struck as soon as he left Highland. Instead, we just sat by and watched as he flew about, as he got closer to us, as we got nearer and nearer to being discovered!"

"You know nothing of time," muttered their leader, his voice calm but slightly threatening. "You think three years is a long time? Ha! I have waited an entire generation for the next Rider to emerge; three years is nothing to me."

"So how much longer will you have us wait? Five years? Seven? Or maybe ten, when he returns to become king? Maybe we should wait another generation? Why? Why have we waited?"

"Because this is a master plan! I don't want to simply succeed; I want to be victorious! I don't want them simply defeated, I want them to be humiliated, irrevocably! And I think three years was the least we could wait to make the wound sting far more sharply."

"So, we will start soon?"

For a moment there was silence.

"Yes," said their leader, a smile slowly spreading across his face. "Yes, I think we have waited long enough. This is the time to come out of hiding and make ourselves known to Highland. First, we shall strike their Rider and then their kingdom!"

The men around the table hailed the news with cheers. Then one spoke, "But now that we are finally to strike, tell us of your plan. How is it that you have found a way to overcome one as powerful as the Dragon Rider, when so many others have failed?"

"Indeed, others have failed," said the leader, his smile widening. "But I have found a way—a dark and powerful secret that has been hidden from the eyes of Tarenthia for nearly two millennia!" The others looked and saw that in his hand he held what appeared to be a medallion. It bore a sickeningly evil design of two snakes curling and entwining themselves around each other and a small emerald embedded in its center. The metal

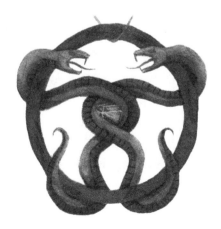

frame appeared dark and tarnished as though from many years of age. The men stared at it, entranced.

"What is it?" breathed one.

"What does it do?" questioned another.

"This," said the leader, "is the Curse. And finally, the time has come to use it. We must move swiftly now. The Rider and his dragon suspect nothing yet, but we must be quick if we are to set the trap at Watergate. The time of the Rider will soon end! The time of a new order has come!"

"To the new order!" yelled the men, raising their fists in the air. "To the new order! And death to the Rider!"

***

Peace sat hunched over the fire in the forest clearing. In the dim light of evening, he could barely make out the glimmer of Ember's green scales from where he lay next to the flickering flames. The night was quiet, though a bit cold, and Peace pulled his cape tightly around him as he stoked the fire.

"So, what did you think of that nation?" he said out loud to Ember.

Dragons are incapable of speaking the human tongue, though they can be taught to understand it. Peace had been teaching Ember so that he would be able to understand those who did not have Links.

I wouldn't call that a nation, snorted Ember. *It was more like a tribe.*

"Wouldn't it at least qualify as a city?" asked Peace with a smile. "After all, they had sturdy houses, farms, horses...what else would they need?"

Walls and towers for a start, retorted Ember. *They had no means of defense, no army, and only primitive weapons.* He shifted his head so that his chin rested more comfortably upon his fore claws and stared idly into the dancing light of the fire as if lost in thought.

"You don't need that to be a city," said Peace. "I'd wish you'd stop judging civilizations by their military. After all, most of what we do doesn't have anything to do with war or conquest."

Perhaps, but then again, it's not that exciting either, said Ember, rolling over halfway.

"Exciting!" said Peace jumping up. "We're helping thousands of people across the entire land! What's not exciting about that?"

It's just that...well...it's nice, and I'm happy to do it, but it's not really that thrilling. There's just no danger in it. Ember rolled back over and his eyes brightened. *I wish we could do something again like that daring escape we had from the Kingdom of Turmoil, or like the avalanche we outflew—do you remember?*

"So," said Peace, "something is only exciting if we face imminent danger of death, is that it?"

Ember snorted quietly and turned his head, looking out into the blackness of the forest. *Well, you have to admit...those times do make better memories.*

Peace smiled. "Right they do, my Eldar."

Suddenly, Ember shifted slightly and cocked his ears. Then he rose to his feet.

What is it? Peace said through the Link.

Someone is coming, Ember answered. They both waited silently for a moment, and then Peace began to discern sounds of footsteps crashing through the forest.

"Who is it?" he hollered. The footsteps grew closer until suddenly a man burst into the clearing, panting heavily.

Peace and Ember waited for him to catch his breath, and then, between gasps, he said, "Rider...we need you...I saw you land...came as soon as I could. My home kingdom...Prosperity...our famed gem...stolen!"

Peace looked at Ember. *You wanted excitement, you said?*

Ember smiled. *Let's go!*

***

Though it was late, they packed up immediately and both men mounted Ember to fly to the kingdom of Prosperity. It wasn't Ember's custom to carry two, but he could do so easily enough over short distances, and Prosperity was not far away.

Once they alighted on the courtyard of the castle, both passengers dismounted and Ember lay down, for he was very tired. Understanding his dragon's weary condition, Peace opted to go to the king and discover the trouble while Ember slept. Ember could feel through the Link that Peace was just as weary, but he accepted the offer and let Peace go alone. Before dropping off to sleep, though, Ember listened as Peace met the king of Prosperity and learned of the situation.

He learned that the kingdom of Prosperity was known across that region of Tarenthia because of a great and valuable emerald it possessed. So great was its splendor, it was not uncommon for people to come from hundreds of miles away just to see the gem. But the previous night another king, Tyrant, had sent spies who snuck into the castle and stole the emerald from the kingdom, killing several of the palace guards in the endeavor. It was believed that it had been taken back to his own kingdom, a citadel named Watergate.

Ember, however, heard no more after that, because his weariness overtook him, and he fell fast asleep.

***

When Peace emerged from the castle, the sky had long since reached the peak of darkness. He smiled at Ember sleeping soundly and lay down next to him. Then he closed his eyes and tried to sleep until morning.

But he was unable to do so; for just before the morning sun began to rise over the hills, he felt himself awoken by a hand that shook him.

"Wake up, Master Rider," someone whispered.

Peace groaned and sat up slowly and stiffly, rubbing his eyes. "What is it? Who are you?"

"I am a messenger from Watergate."

Peace became suddenly more alert. "You? From Watergate? What are you doing here? How did you get in—?"

"Hush," said the man. "I snuck in over the wall. No one in Prosperity knows that I'm here, and I would prefer it to stay that way. I'm here because my king, Tyrant, wants your help."

Peace eyed him curiously. "Why does he need my help? I was told that he stole the gem."

"Yes, that's why he wants to see you. You see that gem first belonged to us, and the king wants to tell you our side of the story before you do anything impulsive."

Peace looked at him oddly. "So, what are you asking me to do?"

"I need you to come with me," said the man. "Come now, before anyone wakes up. I'm afraid they wouldn't let you go otherwise."

Peace considered the request and looked behind him at the sleeping form of Ember. "Let me wake my dragon, and then I'll come."

"No," said the man. "Tyrant desires that you come in good will. If you bring your dragon this time, he might take it as a sign of aggression. I already have a horse saddled to take you to him."

Peace sighed but agreed. He knew that Ember would have been more cautious, but Peace always tried to assume the best of others whenever he could.

"Ok, I'll go with you—just one second."

The man nodded and left.

Peace returned to Ember and, stroking his scales softly, whispered, "Don't worry; I'll be back as soon as I can. Sleep well, my Eldar."

Then he turned and followed the man.

***

Peace was led through the shadows, up to the ramparts of the outer wall, and then down a rope to the other side. There his guide brought him a little way into the woods where two horses stood, saddled and ready. They mounted and traveled east for about an hour until they came to the foot of a large mountain, one in a great range of mountains. The sky was beginning to lighten in the east.

"So, this is the path to Watergate?" asked Peace.

"Yes. Tyrant's kingdom lies inside this ring of mountains. It is a strategic location—there are no valleys or caves that lead through the rock except for one, which is well hidden. Aside from that, there is no other way in, unless you want to go for a long climb."

"Indeed. So where is this secret entrance?"

"Come, I will show you."

The man led Peace to the foot of the mountain, then onto a narrow rocky path that slowly wound its way toward a brilliant waterfall, splashing thunderously down on the rocks from hundreds of feet above. As they got closer, however, Peace saw that the path led not directly toward the waterfall, but rather toward the space between the waterfall and the rock wall behind it. As they got closer still, he noticed that there was no rock wall but rather a large cavern, which seemed to lead directly into the heart of the mountain. Peace smiled when he saw it.

"Ah, you are impressed?" said his guide when he saw the smile.

"Yes, greatly so. The cavern is huge, but the waterfall hides it from every angle unless you are right beside it."

"And now do you understand where our kingdom derives its name?"

"Ah, Watergate! Clever."

Together they passed behind the waterfall and down the long cave, the man's lantern lighting the way. About half an hour later, they reached the end where a similar waterfall blocked the exit. They squeezed between it and the mountain face and emerged on the other side.

"Behold! The kingdom of Watergate!" said the guide, gesturing widely with his arm.

And it was indeed a sight to behold! While the light of the morning sun had not yet made it over the far mountains, the bright moon of the waning night illuminated the kingdom. The city was immense! Peace counted multiple rings of walls encircling a great castle that stood in the distance, and around the entire kingdom great mountains loomed.

"Very impressive!" Peace noted.

His guide led him down another narrow rocky pass toward the bottom of the great mountain ring. Each gate opened for them as they approached and closed behind them as they passed. The man talked as they traveled further into the city.

"That first wall encircles the opening around the waterfall that we came through. This second wall is the true boundary of our Kingdom. Behind it most of our people live and grow our food. Beyond that is an even greater wall, fortified with towers and skylances."

Peace became a bit worried when he heard that. Skylances were giant crossbows designed to shoot tremendous bolts into the air. They were one of the only weapons that served any real threat to a flying dragon.

"What are the skylances for? Have you been attacked by griffins in the past?"

Peace hoped that this was all they were meant for. It was not unusual for wild griffins to attack cities in times past—once they had even been part of a great war against Highland. But they were defeated and later pardoned to serve as messengers. Several of the larger kingdoms trained them for just that purpose. Very few were still wild.

"Oh, no—we've not had any problems with griffins," said his guide with a laugh. "In fact, we've trained several griffins to help defend our city. We keep them in the castle."

Peace became even more concerned. "Then why do you have all these defenses?"

"Oh, mostly just for show. Tyrant is drawn to secure fortresses—creating them is like a hobby to him. Besides, it secures the trust of his subjects."

"So, do you have any real threats from which you require protection?"

"No, not really."

They came to another gateway and passed through.

"Why are you showing me all this?" Peace wondered.

"To display our goodwill. If we meant any evil intent toward you, we wouldn't point out our defenses, would we?"

"I guess I understand," Peace murmured.

They walked on in silence and eventually passed under the fortified wall with the skylances. Up ahead rose the great castle. It looked like a large tower, made of stone and with a gate for its entrance. But they passed right by it. Behind the castle Peace saw a great palace built high-up in the rocky wall of a mountain. They ascended toward it, using carefully cut roads that zigzagged up the steep slope, until they came to the courtyard of the palace—and there, waiting to meet them, was King Tyrant.

***

Ember woke with the sunrise and discovered, to his surprise, that his Rider was not nearby. He got up stiffly, stretched, and looked about for him. Peace didn't seem to be anywhere. Confused, Ember tried to contact him through the Link, but he seemed too far away to find.

Odd, Ember thought.

He began to look around more anxiously; it was not like Peace to leave him so suddenly, with no word. He turned and saw a man walking into the courtyard carrying a bundle of firewood. Ember looked at him curiously.

The man looked back at Ember, confused for a moment, and then, almost as though he could read the question in Ember's eyes, said aloud, "Are you looking for your Rider? He got up early and left this morning. He told me that he was going out for a stroll and that if you woke before he got back you should try hunting a little until he returned."

Ember nodded and the man walked on. *Still strange.*

Spreading his giant wings, Ember leapt from the courtyard and flew over the outer walls of the city. He landed as softly as he could—for many of the villagers were still asleep—on the verge of the forest. *Where could Peace have gone so early?*

"I know where he is."

Ember started. Someone had heard his thoughts, but it wasn't Peace. He looked around in surprise.

Who are you? he asked.

"Don't worry, I mean you no harm."

Ember looked again and this time saw a man coming out of the trees. He was tall and strong, yet something about him was youthful and energetic. He wore a sword at his side and a Link around his neck.

Where did you get that? asked Ember, defensively. He had never known of anyone aside from the King, the Rider, and their dragons owning Links.

The stranger held out his hand and bowed in respect.

"The King gave it to me. When he was the Rider, and I was but a boy, I was able to help him out of a bit of trouble. To show his gratitude, he gave me my own Link when he took the throne. He knew that I loved dragons and wanted to be able to communicate with them."

The man reached out a hand as if to touch Ember's scales. Ember moved away and eyed him coldly.

I've never heard of something like that happening before. What is your name?

The man withdrew his hand. "You're right; you probably wouldn't have heard of it happening before—it's a very rare honor. And my name is Dep."

Dep? That is an odd name.

"Well, it's not my full name, but that's of little importance. More importantly, I've come to warn you; both you and your Rider are in terrible danger."

Ember looked the man over suspiciously. *Danger? How?*

"I think someone is plotting against you. Three days ago, a group of eight men snuck into the city disguised as merchants. I was curious, so I followed and heard them talking about you, and Peace, and some sort of plot involving Watergate. I couldn't hear more details without being noticed, so the next day I went to learn more and found that several of

them had returned to Watergate. This, by the way, was around the same time the emerald was stolen."

You think they were the ones responsible?

"I can't say anything for sure; but I think they may be working with Tyrant. If so, I would be concerned. I saw one of those men wake Peace before the dawn and convince him to go to Watergate alone."

What? growled Ember. There must be a mistake. Why would Peace go to Watergate without me?

"Is it his habit to think of his safety first?"

No, Ember admitted. He's not one to instinctively suspect danger. Sometimes he can be far too trusting. But still—I was told that he had only gone for a walk.

"Who told you that?"

A man; just a man in the courtyard.

"Did he have a beard and black hair?"

Ember eyed him with surprise. Yes! How could you know?

"Because one of the men who stayed behind has a beard and black hair. If this is the case, then this could very well be a trap! Why else would they convince Peace to leave you, and then lie to you about it?"

Ember shook his head. No, you must be mistaken. No one would dare plot against the Dragon Rider. He paused for a second, then growled softly. But then again...

"Trust me, I know what I heard; you should go now and look for him. If this turns out to be a mistake, all will be well. But if it is a trap, you must hurry because they will not be expecting you to have caught on."

Yes, you are right. I must hurry, agreed Ember, looking toward the skies.

Dep nodded. "Then fly fast, my friend. The kingdom of Watergate is in that direction, in the center of the range of mountains. I wish you good luck!"

He held out his hand again to touch Ember in a gesture of farewell.

But Ember was already facing toward the mountains and spreading his wings, his mind focused on his master.

***

Peace was led into Tyrant's giant throne room with many nobles entering behind him. He walked to the center and watched as people stood around him, and as the king ascended to his throne. Once seated, Tyrant turned to look toward Peace and eyed with intrigue the blade that he carried.

"Well, isn't this ironic," he said. "Peace with a sword. Funny that those things should exist together."

"Ah," said Peace, "but it's not ironic at all; for many times it is the sword that brings peace, and almost always the sword keeps it."

"Well said, very well said," acknowledged the king. "I hope, though, that we will not need one to bring about peace here."

"I should hope not."

"I do prefer peace, you know. I hate it when things have to come to the sword."

"If that is truly what you believe, then why did you steal the emerald from Prosperity?"

"We did not steal anything!" said the king bitterly. "That gem has always been ours! It was mined in these very mountains!"

"Then how is it that the kingdom of Prosperity has been in possession of it for so many years?"

"Because it was the thieving scoundrels in Prosperity who did the stealing. Many, many years ago we discovered the emerald while we were still building our city. We have been mining since we first settled here, but that emerald was the largest gem ever found. It was the joy of our entire kingdom! People would gather from miles around to gaze on its beauty, and Watergate was never more prosperous.

"The kingdom of Prosperity, however, was jealous. One year we had a great jousting tournament with them, and our champions fought theirs for greater and greater prizes. Then, when the stakes were at their highest, the king of Prosperity said that he would fight me himself for the jewel of Watergate. I did not know what to do. I could not back down from such a challenge in front of my people, so I accepted.

"But then—treachery! For as I rode toward him and he toward me, a soldier of Prosperity raised his shield and reflected the sun directly into my eyes, blinding me so that I was knocked off my horse. I challenged the match as unfair and asked that it should be replayed, but the king of Prosperity demanded that we give him the emerald nonetheless."

Tyrant rested his chin on his fist, obviously angry over what had happened. "For nearly twenty years I longed to bring it back here, where it rightfully belonged. So, when a group of men came to me and offered to get it back in return for certain favors, well, how could I do anything else but give my approval?"

"Why did you never come to Highland with this dispute?"

"You people never would've understood. And the king of Prosperity is a liar. The king of Highland would not have believed me. But you believe me don't you; now that you have been here and seen for yourself?"

Peace considered the situation silently. "I think it would be best," he said at last, "if you give me the emerald."

"What! Why? It's mine! I cannot give it up again."

"Yes, but I think it best that I hear the story of the tournament from both sides before making any decisions. If the gem rightfully belongs to you, you have my word that it will be returned to you."

"No!" shouted Tyrant, rising from his throne. "I have no desire to regain it through negotiations; this is a time for war! I didn't bring you here so you could hear my story and then go and decide who the gem belongs to. I brought you here because I need your help to destroy Prosperity for taking what is mine!"

Peace took a step back. "You can't be serious. Just a moment ago you said how much you hate bloodshed. None of this requires—"

"War? It most certainly does! They stole that emerald and with it our fame and prestige! For twenty years they kept what was rightfully mine, and it is my intention to make them pay for every day they kept it!"

Peace backed up further and, without realizing it, placed his hand on his sword hilt.

The king didn't seem to notice. "But we need you, Rider. With you, the war will be quick and decisive, and we can finally end this injustice! I want you to fight alongside me."

Peace was now seriously thinking about the sword his hand rested on. He did not like the direction the situation was heading, but he summoned his courage and looked Tyrant straight in the eye. "I have no intention of starting a war—especially when no investigation has been made."

The king stared straight back at him. His face was cold and menacing. "I suggest you join us Rider. If you don't, we may have to insist."

***

Ember breathed heavily and his wings beat furiously as he climbed higher through the thin air. He flew towards an opening between the mountain peaks ahead, and beyond that, by the new light of the cold morning, he could faintly make out the kingdom of Watergate. Every few moments he tried to contact Peace, but every time he was unable to find him.

He flew harder. *I hope I can make it in time.*

He hoped that he would; he hoped that it was all a mistake, and that Peace was in no real danger. But there was a sharp doubt pricking his mind.

Where are you, my Eldar?

***

Peace had his sword drawn now, but Tyrant didn't seem to notice. He was walking across the room, advancing on him.

"Why?" he growled. "Why can't you see that this is what needs to be done? You are the Rider; you are supposed to keep the peace throughout the land."

"Yes, but your plan will not bring that," said Peace firmly.

"Would you leave this great injustice unpunished?" shouted the king.

"It is not worthy of war."

"Fine then! I see we need to do things my way."

Instantly, all the nobles in the room threw off their cloaks, revealing themselves to be soldiers. More than ten drew swords, and behind them several more raised loaded crossbows.

"I really do hate it when negotiations fail," said Tyrant. "It always makes things so much harder. Now I suggest that unless you have some legendary skill with that sword of yours, you drop it."

Peace did not have any such skills—fencing had never been his greatest subject—so he eyed the situation carefully and slowly placed his sword on the ground.

"By doing this," Peace said slowly, "you are declaring war on Highland. Are you sure that this is what you desire?"

Tyrant laughed. "I do not fear Highland or its King," he said. "And besides, I think that they will be far more...understanding, when they see that your life is in my hands."

Two of the soldiers grabbed Peace roughly by the arms; another picked up his sword, and a fourth took his Link.

But Peace looked the king in the eye and said, "You will never get away with this. You know that don't you? No one has ever risen up against my father and won."

"But *I shall!*" yelled Tyrant. "I have *you!* This moment marks the beginning of a new era, a new order! Nothing can stop me now!"

"Sire!" shouted a man, running into the chamber. "Sire! It's the dragon! He's here!"

"What! The dragon? Here?" cried the king, hurrying to the giant window behind his throne. His eyes widened as he saw the dark spot in the sky soaring over the mountains. "Impossible! He wasn't to suspect anything until sunset! How can this be?"

"Perhaps they have learned of our plans," said one of the soldiers.

"If they have," gasped another, "then this changes everything!"

"This changes nothing!" thundered Tyrant, stepping forward and grabbing Peace by the shoulders. "Listen to me!" he growled. "I want you to contact your dragon and tell him that if he values your life, he must land and surrender himself immediately."

"No!" bristled Peace. "I will never deliver him into your hands!"

"Let me put it another way," said Tyrant, breathing heavily. "I have every skylance in my kingdom set toward him right now. My griffins are also standing by. If he does not surrender himself, he will be shot down—and if somehow he makes it through, you will be killed."

"How do you expect me to contact him without my Link?"

"What kind of fool do you think I am? Links receive thoughts; he will hear you. You just won't hear him, which will discourage any funny business."

"Tyrant, no; don't do this."

"Do as I command you!"

* * *

Ember was nearing the castle when he heard the voice through his Link. *Ember,* it said. *I need you to land...*

Peace, it's you! Are you all right?

...Surrender yourself to Tyrant's soldiers...

Peace, what's wrong?

...Do it immediately. Just trust me on this...

Ember shook his head in disbelief.

Peace! Where are you? Are you captured?

...He says that if you do not land in the castle courtyard immediately, he will kill us both. I promise everything will work out...just please land and do what he says...

Ember couldn't believe what he was hearing.

Peace...? he asked in vain.

Then he shook his head and roared so loudly that it echoed off the mountains. In his mind he could still hear his Rider's monologue, telling him to land, to not be afraid.

Please..., Ember asked beseechingly into the wind. *Please just tell me if you're all right; have they hurt you?*

But Peace did not hear him.

You're almost out of time. Land now. Don't worry, you'll be all right. We both will be; just don't resist for now.

Ember roared again with rage and threw himself into a dive toward the ground. He saw the courtyard and the men there waiting to take him prisoner. He dove harder, his rage overtaking him. When he landed, the ground shook and the mountains rumbled with the echo. The men backed up momentarily, but then rushed toward him.

Don't resist them, said Peace. *Tyrant says that if you do, we'll both pay for it. Just do whatever they tell you; I promise that...*

Just then one of the men seized Ember's Link, and he heard no more.

***

Peace watched helplessly from the window, Tyrant's sword at his throat, as the men swarmed his dragon. "Please," he said. "Please don't harm him."

"Ha!" said Tyrant, chuckling. "I don't think you're in any position to ask that."

Two of the guards began to drag Peace away.

"Take him to the dungeons!" yelled Tyrant. "And lock the dragon in the underground prison we designed. Let's see if a few days of starvation will begin to tame him."

He laughed wildly at the ceiling. "The new order has come!"

***

For a day and a half, Ember languished in the dark prison under the earth. His cell was built specifically for a dragon of his size. It was several hundred feet underground, the walls were pure rock, and the iron gate across the doorway could withstand a hurricane.

Ember stood in the center of the cell, muzzled, with his great wings pinned to his sides and each leg fastened to the walls with reinforced chains. From the way he was bound, Ember could not lie down, and he could not rest. It was also pitch black, for not even the slightest ray of light penetrated the deep darkness.

He felt eternity after eternity pass as he stood helpless, enduring agony of both body and mind. He had no way to keep track of time. Had he been there an hour? A day? A century? No one came to him. No one spoke to him. No food was delivered. How long had it been since he had last eaten? Yesterday? The day before? Certainly not since they arrived at Prosperity, and that seemed a millennium ago. He could not bear it. His hunger tortured him to no end.

There was no word on what was happening above. Maybe they had killed Peace. No, he was too valuable. They could not have killed him. But why the silence? What were they doing to him? Had he been beaten? Tortured? No! Ember desperately tried to calm his inner anguish of heart.

He must not allow himself to think of these horrors. They wouldn't have. They couldn't have. Peace had to be all right. He had to!

Ember whined and shook his head. The madness seemed to be growing inside his mind. *Eldar, where are you?* he begged.

But still there was no answer.

3

The Escape

There was a commotion—a sound in the stillness—that brought Ember out of his deepening insanity. He heard a thud and the clattering of a sword hitting the ground. Ember shook his large head and strained in vain to see through the darkness. Was it one of the guards?

Suddenly there was the cry of a soldier, and another sword hit the ground. Then someone spoke.

"Ember!" It was a voice that he immediately recognized.

Dep? he called out. *If Dep still had his Link, he would be able to hear him. Dep!*

"It's all right, I'm here."

Ember breathed a sigh of relief. There was a glimmer around the corner outside his cell, and then a man holding a blinding lantern emerged. Ember quickly turned his head away from the sharp light.

"Sorry," said Dep, lowering a shade on it. The glow decreased.

What are you doing here? asked Ember, looking back. His joy was practically overcoming him. *I thought you lived in Prosperity.*

"I don't; in fact, I don't live around here at all. My home is actually a castle by the sea, nearly three days' journey east of here." The man pulled out a ring of large keys that he had taken from one of the guards. "I'm actually an ambassador to this city; I only stopped at Prosperity first to rest."

He squeezed between the bars of the gate (which were designed for dragons, not people) and started to unchain each of Ember's legs.

How long have I been down here? asked Ember after a few moments.

"From what I can tell, I'd say almost two days. It's evening now." Dep finished with the fourth chain and Ember sank to the ground, exhausted from standing so long. Dep climbed up onto his back to work on the chain holding his wings.

"I can't believe what they have done to you," he said with deep sadness in his voice. "I have always loved dragons—I never imagined that I would see one treated this way." He finished releasing Ember's wings and slid down off his back. "Here, bend your head down so I can get your muzzle off."

Ember did so obediently, and Dep began to cut the straps with his knife.

Tell me, said Ember, preparing to ask the question that had been burning in his mind. *Is Peace all right?*

Dep sighed and placed his hand on Ember's forehead between his eyes. For some reason, Ember found an enormous comfort in his touch. He wished that he might keep his hand there forever.

"He is," said Dep. "He's perfectly fine, though I'm not sure he will stay that way for long. Tyrant just summoned him to his palace, and I think he's going to force Peace to help them take over Prosperity, and perhaps Highland too."

Dep took his hand away and finished pulling the muzzle off. "I can't help Peace, but maybe you can. Fly to the palace and get him out of there;

I know that you're not in good condition for this, but you're his only hope."

He took the keys over to the great iron gate and unlocked it. "Here Ember, I need your help; it's too heavy for me to push alone."

Ember struggled weakly to his feet and shoved it open on its creaky hinges. *Will you be all right?* he asked.

"Me? I'll be fine. No one who saw me come down here has lived to tell the tale. They don't suspect me of knowing anything. But hurry, you must go as quickly as you can. As soon as they see that you've escaped,

they may threaten Peace's life again to control you. You must catch them off guard."

I will go. Thank you. I am indebted to you for your help; Highland will remember your great service and will honor you.

"They already have," said Dep touching his Link. "But go; the tunnel opening is that way. Good luck, my friend."

And good luck to you as well.

***

Peace stood in Tyrant's throne room once again, this time as a prisoner. His hands were unbound, but he had no weapon and the many guards and crossbowmen in the room made his captivity perfectly clear. With limited patience, Peace stood listening to the king's endless stream of monologues as to why he should join them.

"Look, Rider, you were brought here because you were supposed to see reason. You were supposed to see what was right and help us uphold it. Can you not see what this world has become? It is a dictatorship! Every country here lives under the dark shadow of Highland; one cannot live or prosper unless your King sees fit."

"My King," said Peace with suppressed anger, "only limits kingdoms when it is best for them. They must all follow the wisdom of Highland, or freedom as we know it across this land will die."

"Freedom?" Tyrant spat. "How is following rules freedom? If your King wants us to be truly free, he will allow us to make our own decrees and choose our own standards. If one country goes to war against another, why should they be held back by some distant regime? Mark my words, I *will* destroy Prosperity for what they've done to me whether you're with me or not. But when we rise up against Highland—"

"I will never join you to destroy my own homeland."

"But you could save lives! If I fight alone, thousands will die, and innocent people will be slain in the crossfire. But with you, they would surrender immediately. That's all it would take—no death, no bloodshed, no one would even have to draw a sword. Isn't that what you want? Don't you want *peace*?"

"Destroying Highland will plunge all of Tarenthia into turmoil! You have no idea what devastation this will bring upon us."

"Anything would be better than the way things are now!" Tyrant exclaimed.

There was a moment of silence, and then the king walked behind his throne to the great window that overlooked his kingdom.

"Peace," he said. "When I look out on Watergate, I see a thriving nation; a nation that has flourished and become well-known. I want them to prosper and become a great people. I want what is best for them. I want them to be..."

His voice trailed off—immediately he spun around with fear in his eyes.

"Get down!" he yelled, running across the room. "Get down!"

The soldiers all ducked instinctively as Tyrant charged toward Peace, knocking him to the marble floor.

Suddenly, the great window exploded in a shower of glistening fragments and the palace shook as though a meteor had struck. Peace pushed Tyrant away and struggled to his feet, looking behind the throne at the window which had now become a gaping hole.

"Ember!" he shouted with astonishment.

The dragon had crashed hard with the force of his own momentum and was struggling to get on his feet, shaking his head. Peace could see it took him several tries. The guards around the room began to pick themselves up, warily keeping their distance. A brave one fired a crossbow, glancing an arrow off the scales of Ember's snout. The dragon looked around, annoyed, and blasted fire in the direction the arrow had come from. Then he looked back, searching for his Rider through the dust.

"Ember!" Peace shouted again, and this time the dragon immediately spotted him. Without their Links, Peace could not hear Ember, but he could see in his dragon's eyes overwhelming joy.

"I knew that no prison could keep you!" Peace laughed.

Ember lurched toward him, and Peace stepped forward to meet his companion. Suddenly he felt the hands of soldiers grab him and the cold steel of a sword at his throat.

"Stop!" yelled Tyrant to the oncoming dragon. "Stop right there or I'll kill him where he stands!"

Ember immediately stopped dead cold, and the joy in his eyes was replaced by horror and fear.

Tyrant looked about angrily at his men. "What is this!" he screamed with rage. "How did he get out? Who let him escape?"

"Perhaps dragons are a little harder to contain than you thought," said Peace with a smirk.

Tyrant laughed nervously. "Easy to contain? Ha! They're easier to contain than humans!"

Brandishing the sword, he held at Peace's throat, he turned to Ember.

"You stupid beast!" he hollered. "You managed to break out of a dungeon that I was assured was completely inescapable, blast your way into my palace, throw my men into disarray—but find yourself stopped short by a king with a knife."

He laughed again, regaining full confidence in himself.

"Now," he said, "you will leave here at once, and return to your prison cell; or your precious Rider will die here and now. Your little escapade is already going to cost him dearly; you wouldn't want it to cost him his life as well, now would you?"

Ember looked fleetingly back and forth between Tyrant and Peace. He began to back away, looking beseechingly toward his master for help.

"Wait!" shouted Peace. The tension in the room was high, but oddly enough, he was smiling smugly. "Don't you dare leave this room," he said to Ember, who paused obediently.

"Who do you think you are?" yelled Tyrant, turning to him. "I'm the one giving the orders here!"

"You know," said Peace with a smile. "Perhaps you'd like to think through your situation a bit more before you make any rash decisions."

"What are you talking about?"

"Think through, for example, the fact that there stands before you a great fire-breathing dragon in the prime of its youth. Consider furthermore, that you have made this dragon both very hungry and very angry. And that given the chance, he would no doubt be inclined to burn down this entire palace and maybe even the rest of your precious kingdom that you care so much for. The *only* reason he holds back is because there is one person in this entire nation whom he cares enough about to stay his rage."

"That's exactly my point! That's why—"

"—And you actually expect us to believe," interrupted Peace, triumph rising in his voice. "that you would be willing to murder this very person *right in front of him?*"

The room went silent. It went silent for several seconds. Tyrant looked threateningly at Peace, incomparable fury and rage showing on his face. But the Rider continued smiling, for he could see the veins in the king's forehead throbbing.

When at last Tyrant spoke, his voice was dark and menacing. "I was only planning on killing you if he did not obey."

"And what if he doesn't?" Peace shot back confidently. "Suppose he doesn't leave; will you follow through? Because I don't think you can do it. I don't think you have the courage."

"I do! I can kill you, and I will!"

"Then do it," retorted Peace.

Ember looked at him in shock, and even Tyrant seemed stunned.

"Go on," he continued. "My dragon hasn't left, so go ahead—kill me and sentence yourself and your kingdom to death!"

Tyrant yelled and swung his sword back to cut off the Rider's head. Ember jolted and roared in fear.

But Peace was not afraid, for he saw in Tyrant's eyes, behind his anger, a deathly fear for his own life. Ember might have been easy to control because he loved his Rider, but Tyrant was easier still for he loved only himself.

The sword hung in the air for several seconds, but then Tyrant slowly brought it to his side. His rage was still clear, but now there was obvious fear mixed in.

"So, what do you want? What point are you trying to make?" he asked. His voice was low and shaking.

"I only mean to say that we are at an impasse," said Peace. "Ember will not try to kill you, for he knows that your last act will be to kill me out of revenge; but he also will not leave, for he knows that you will not follow through with your threat. Therefore, I suggest a compromise.

"If you meet our demands, and if you drop this whole business of war, then I will give you my word as a Rider that we will both leave without hurting anyone and this entire city will be left unharmed. Furthermore, I also promise that if you release us right now, we will forgive you everything you've done to us, and forget this entire little incident. We will only concern ourselves with that which was our concern at the first—the ownership of the emerald."

Tyrant's eyes shifted back and forth between Peace, Ember, and his men standing around him. It was clear that he was reluctant to back down in front of his subjects.

"Trust me," said Peace. "Not many are offered mercy such as this."

Tyrant's eyes shifted back and forth a little bit more, but then he placed his sword on the ground.

"What are your demands?"

Ember visibly relaxed, and the tension in the room seemed to die down. Peace was pleased.

"First," he said, "I want our Links back."

"You!" yelled Tyrant to the nearest soldier. "Go and get the Links."

The soldier, no doubt happy to be out of the room that held an angry dragon, immediately ran for the doors.

"Second," continued Peace, "I want my sword."

"Get his sword too!" Tyrant yelled after the soldier.

"And finally, I want the emerald."

Tyrant's face fell and his eyes narrowed.

"But...didn't you hear what I said earlier? I thought you understood that it rightfully belongs to us."

"If that is the case, I promise you will get it back."

The king looked around desperately, as if searching for a way out, but finally bowed his head.

"Someone go...go and get the emerald," he said without looking up.

Another soldier headed off and Tyrant looked at Peace beseechingly. "I hope you do return it to us—I hope you do what is right."

"I promise you, I will," said Peace confidently.

The first soldier came back in, carrying the Links on a jeweled pillow.

"Ah, here we are!" said the king as he took them. "I do hope that you forgive us for what we've done to you," he said, placing one Link around Peace's neck.

Then he took the other and walked slowly over to Ember.

"It really wasn't my idea anyway. It was the people that came—they put me up to it." He held the Link up to Ember, who growled softly at him before lowering his head.

"Tell me," continued Tyrant, with no trace of emotion in his voice. "These allow you to hear each other's thoughts, but do they also allow you to sense the other's feelings?"

"Yes," said Peace. "They transmit all thoughts and emotions."

"Good," said the king, letting the Link's chain fall around Ember's neck. "Then feel his pain!"

With a sudden flourish, Tyrant whipped a red dagger from the folds of his cloak and stabbed Ember in the chest. Instantly the dragon roared and fell to the ground in the grip of fiery agony. Peace, wearing the Link, also collapsed with the torture of the wound running through him. The blade had not been long enough to reach Ember's heart, but the fire persisted and seemed to spread out across his back, wings, legs, even to the tip of his tail.

"What have you done to him?" cried Peace, clutching his own heart as though he were the one injured.

Tyrant laughed and flung his bloodied dagger across the floor where it bounced and landed at Peace's feet.

"It's my own design!" he exclaimed, a ruthless grin across his face. "A dagger with a hollow blade and a hole in its tip, meant to be filled with poison or venom. Once the victim has been stabbed, pushing on the top of the hilt injects its contents."

Across the room, Ember continued to roll about screeching and thrashing with pain, his tail striking against the stones.

"Is that what you did? You poisoned him?"

"Oh no," said Tyrant, pulling another dagger, this one blue, from his cloak. "Poison isn't fast enough. I needed something that would take effect immediately."

He held up the second dagger in triumph. "No, *this* one has poison in it. The red one had something similar to a virus. I discovered it when my griffins first contracted it; it gave them tremendous pain for nearly three days until it wore off. It was so bad in fact, that I thought I'd keep it on hand just for cases like this. Of course, I didn't know for certain that it would work on dragons, but I was willing to take a chance."

He looked toward Ember on the floor, still crying out and too delirious to notice Tyrant approach him holding his dagger high.

"It is fun to watch him suffer, is it not? But unfortunately, he has proven himself too hard to contain and too dangerous to keep alive. Perhaps we should get rid of him now while we have the chance."

Smiling wickedly, the king raised the poisoned dagger above his head to strike at the fevered dragon's heart. Peace screamed out and, with a burst of strength, threw off the guards holding him, grabbed the red dagger at his feet, and rushed forward.

Instantly every crossbow in the room was leveled at him, but instead of taking notice Peace fell to his knees, still several feet away from both dragon and king.

He shouted, "Stop! Stop right now, or I'll kill myself!"

The room went silent at once; Tyrant looked at him curiously.

"Do you want to run that one by me again?" he asked, dagger still poised to strike.

Peace pointed the red blade at his own heart. "I said that if you kill him, I will kill myself."

Tyrant was incredulous. "Is...is that supposed to be a threat? Why should I care? And why should I believe that you would ever do something like that?"

"I would do it," said Peace gravely, "because I love that dragon more than anything else in the world; and if you take him from me, my life will not be worth living anymore. And as for why you should care, maybe you'd like to consider the fact that my father is the King of Highland and my brother is Justice. If we do not return to them, they will track us back to you, and without either of our lives to barter how do you expect to keep them from destroying you and your entire kingdom?"

Tyrant started at him even more incredulously, if that were possible, wondering how it could be that he was always the one holding the blade, yet never the one calling the shots. The veins in his forehead throbbed again, and he backed away from the fevered dragon.

"You would really kill yourself over him? Over a creature?"

"He's far more than just a creature to me."

"You're lying! You won't kill yourself. Grieved and saddened you might be, but you won't take your own life."

"You have no idea what it means to be bonded to a dragon."

Now Tyrant was the one smiling. "All right, fine. If that's the way you want it, go right ahead. If he means so much that you'd kill yourself, then prove it!"

"I will."

Peace... came Ember's voice weakly through the Link. Please...please don't.

"Do it!" shouted Tyrant. No doubt he was expecting another battle of will, similar to the one he had gone through. Instead, Peace, without hesitation, plunged the dagger into his flesh.

No! cried Ember as he saw his Rider slump to the ground. The stab of the dagger which rolled through the Link seemed to drown all his pain. With a roar he leapt to his feet, knocking Tyrant over, and staggered across the room toward his fallen comrade. Crossbows fired upon him, but the bolts only bounced off the scales of his back as he curled himself around Peace's fallen body. He felt rage and despair overtake him and he blasted fire all around, causing many of the guards to drop their weapons and flee.

Then he felt a voice. *Great show; but let's not overdo it.*

Ember looked down at Peace in shock and found him alive and laughing. Then he saw that Peace had not stabbed himself in the heart but rather in his left arm.

Great show? You're one to talk! I thought you were dead!

I only said I would kill myself if they killed you. He asked me to prove it, so I showed him my resolve. I also thought that perhaps the shock would wake you up. Good thing it worked.

Peace quickly rose, ignoring his pain, and grabbed two bolts off the floor along with a loaded crossbow someone had dropped.

"Stop them!" cried Tyrant, who was now hiding behind his overturned throne. "Somebody, stop them!" Soldiers started running in at them.

Are you able to fly? Peace asked.

Ember staggered; the pain, combined with his hunger and weakness were beginning to overcome his adrenaline. *I'm not sure.*

Well, you must try, said Peace. *We must get you out of here.*

Holding his weapons under his right arm, Peace limped over to Ember and pulled himself up onto his back. Ember struggled to his feet and with a roar lurched his way to the broken window, leaping through it. He spread his wings to break his dive, and immediately pain hit him like a tidal wave.

"You can do it, Ember!" cried Peace over the wind, and he placed his hand on his dragon's back.

Ember felt both comfort and strength from his touch, and managed to level out, banking hard to avoid the castle which loomed directly in front of them.

"Head to the other end of the city!" Peace called out, and Ember shakily obeyed.

Behind them there was the sound of a trumpet and two griffins flew up from the ground, their feathers glistening in the setting sun. Peace took aim with the crossbow and fired. It is not an easy thing to shoot with one arm from the back of a flying dragon, but Peace managed a lucky shot. He hit one of the griffins in the wing and it plummeted toward the ground with a screech.

I don't know if I can keep this up, came Ember's voice.

He was panting hard now, due to the dagger wound in his chest, and Peace could feel the jolt of pain that went through him with every beat of his heart. Peace rubbed his back again.

The other griffin began to gain on them. Quickly, Peace attempted to reload his crossbow, which was not an easy feat.

"Keep going! We're almost there!" he shouted, aiming his weapon again.

He fired, but at that moment Ember jolted and the bolt went astray. He struggled to reload his last arrow.

I'm not going...to make it...over the mountains, heaved Ember.

Looking forward, Peace saw that they were indeed approaching the mountains which surrounded Watergate. He turned back and tried to aim.

"Head for that waterfall in front of you. There's a tunnel behind it."

Are you...sure?

Peace turned his whole body around backwards to better face the griffin, which was almost upon them. He raised his crossbow again.

"Yes, I've seen it; trust me!"

With the last of his strength, Ember dove toward the waterfall just as the griffin spread out its claws to stab his wing. Peace fired as they passed through the wall of water, and suddenly they were enveloped in the blackness of the tunnel. He never knew whether or not he had hit the griffin, but regardless, it did not follow them. He leaned back against Ember's neck in relief as the dragon made a crash landing on the cave floor.

"We did it!" he shouted, and his voice echoed all around them.

We...we made it? gasped Ember, struggling to catch his breath.

"Yes, we did," said Peace, jumping unsteadily to the ground.

He rubbed the dragon's neck gently and waited a few moments, listening as his laborious breathing echoed off the cave walls.

Finally, he spoke, "We can't stay here. At the end of this tunnel is another waterfall and, beyond that, the forest. We'll find someplace to hide there, and then maybe we can begin to recover."

It was several minutes before Ember was able to regain his feet, for his stay in the dungeon, the wound in his chest, and the virus within him all seemed to be hammering upon him at once. When they did finally manage to make it out of the tunnel, his flight was very slow and arduous.

As the sun set, however, and as the stars came out, they were able to make it to the concealment of a small forest clearing before Ember's strength gave out entirely. Peace let him rest for a good deal of the night while he bandaged his arm, made a fire, and kept watch.

Eventually however, as the stars began to fade and a new sunrise began to grow on the horizon, Ember awoke and asked the question that had been on Peace's mind all night.

So, what will we do now, Rider?

I'll have to make a trip to Prosperity. Hopefully, they'll have something for you to eat, along with some friendly griffins that will send a message back to Highland for us.

You mean to bring the King into this? questioned Ember. *It's against tradition for us to ask his aid. We are supposed to face the troubles we encounter without his help.*

Then I will send for my brother, Justice. Normally I would try to reconcile this dispute myself, but Tyrant has declared a deadly threat against the kingdom of Prosperity, and we are in no condition to defend them alone. We will need all the help we can get.

Ember nodded. *You are right; Justice must come.*

4

The Defeat

"This is outrageous! You promised destruction upon the Rider!"

"Patience; plans take time."

"Your plan failed! They have escaped, and now war is upon us!"

Once again, the men were sitting around a wooden table, with the light of the full moon streaming through the window; only this time the meeting took place in the castle of Watergate. Once again, their leader sat in the shadows, but this time his associates were furious with him.

"My plan has not failed," he said.

"Not failed? Look around!" demanded one man. "We went through great effort to trap the Rider and contain him just as you said. But someone tipped off his dragon and they still got away! You said your dungeon would hold a dragon, but you were wrong! Your plan is coming to pieces and now you ask for patience? How many more must fall before you have victory?" He gestured to the three empty seats at the table.

"My dungeon design was perfect!" barked the leader. "It was impossible to escape. No, my friends, he had *help*; the soldiers guarding him were slain by a sword. Someone appears to be meddling in our scheme."

"So, the master plan that you've been working on for over a decade has been found out!"

"I have men working on this problem, and I can assure you that we now know the identity of this...person. He will not interfere any longer."

"But it's too late; your plan failed! Due to your incompetence, they both escaped us."

"It was that bumbling king that let them escape, not I! And besides, do you really think that I don't have a backup plan?"

"It's too late for backup plans. The armies of Highland will soon be upon us; we have no time for another trap—we are at war!"

"And do you think that war is *not* what I want?"

The men around the table grew silent and listened with renewed attention.

"War is a machine, a powerful, grinding machine," said the leader. "With a little push, I can make it serve whatever end I need!"

He had their interest now. Those who were shouting against him only seconds before were now rethinking their questions.

"War is my tool, and with it I shall carve out the destruction of both Rider and King. My plan has not failed, it has only just begun! The new order will reign!"

"The new order will reign!" shouted the men in unison.

"To the new order!"

"To the new order! And death to the Rider!"

***

Peace got up slowly from the castle courtyard, stretched, and walked along the wall toward the military camp. He went around a corner and through an archway before he came upon the tents, for he had asked that they not disturb Ember on the courtyard while he was recovering.

All around him soldiers were marching or feeding horses or looking over maps—all things to be expected from an army that had only just arrived at Prosperity a few days ago and had already taken part in a great battle. Peace once again felt for the bandage covering his self-inflicted wound on his arm as he looked around. He strode up to a distinguished man who was overseeing the soldiers.

"Justice, my brother! How are things? How did your little campaign go against the invading force yesterday?"

His brother turned to face him. He looked grim and serious as usual, but he smiled slightly when he saw Peace. "Little? Little campaign indeed. We routed the entire army!"

"Really? You've defeated them already?"

"Aye; while you've been sleeping, I've been hard at work organizing this kingdom's pitiful band of soldiers along with my own horsemen. Apparently, our attack caught them off guard; when they caught sight of Highland's soldiers, and when they saw me, they broke rank and fled. We chased many back to Watergate and the rest we captured."

"Fantastic! I couldn't have asked for a better general."

"Thank you; I am glad that I got here in time."

Above them, they heard great wings beating the air, and a moment later Ember landed next to them, shaking the ground slightly.

Is there anything that I missed? he asked, as he laid down on the grass to rest in a more comfortable position. The virus still lingered within him, but he had almost fully recovered.

Not much, said Peace through the Link, *except that Justice here just chased off the whole Watergate army.*

Oh, he did, did he? said Ember sleepily, closing his eyes. *Too bad I wasn't there to help.*

"We've also captured three particular men," said Justice, after he sensed that their silent conversation was finished.

"What three men?" asked Peace.

"Apparently they are three accomplices to whomever put Tyrant up to this whole plot."

"You think someone else is behind it?"

"Almost certainly. I know Tyrant well enough to say that he never would've done something as bold as trying to capture the Dragon Rider on his own. He's too cowardly and fears too much for his own life. I think that he's working with someone and these three men appear to know about it—although they aren't talking."

"If they were working with Tyrant, then what were they doing here?"

"It seems they played a part in the trap against you. I suspect that we will find more when we invade Watergate."

Peace suddenly looked stunned. "What? Invade Watergate?"

"Yes, of course. Their army is scattered, and ours is in fair condition; now is the perfect time to start our counterattack."

"Counterattack? I asked you to come here to protect Prosperity, not start a war."

"But they have directly defied the rule of Highland. They must pay the price for their rebellion."

"No, it needn't come to this. Hundreds of innocent people will die! We...we can try reasoning with them; we can try to negotiate with Tyrant!"

Because we all know how well that worked out last time, snorted Ember without opening his eyes.

Peace glared at him, but Justice, even without hearing the dragon, seemed to be of the same opinion.

"I think they have made clear what they think of diplomacy," he said. "And their crimes are too great to go unpunished. Let's recap—so far, Tyrant has lured both of you into a trap and mistreated you severely; he said he would let you go and then broke his promise; he threatened your life and tried to take Ember's; he sent his soldiers against Prosperity; and he declared a clear threat against Highland. Did I miss anything?"

Well, he stole an emerald, suggested Ember.

"Be quiet!" Peace hissed back sharply and, quite by mistake, out loud.

Justice smiled. "Ah, so he agrees with me?" he guessed. "I wouldn't blame him if he did; how can you withhold justice from someone who deserves it when it is within your power to act? He sees this situation clearly."

Peace groaned, but in the end was forced to agree. The only clear course of action they could take was to retaliate; it was one of the responsibilities that came with being a Rider. But he agreed only halfheartedly, for Peace hated war.

***

The attack commenced the next day. With Ember scouting ahead and Justice commanding the army, they reached the waterfall that led into Watergate by mid-afternoon.

At first it was nearly impossible to capture the tunnel, for Tyrant had many bowmen stationed there. After several failed attempts, Peace was at last forced to fly over the mountains and take the cavern from the other side, allowing enough soldiers to get through to gain a foothold. The defenders retreated behind their walls, and Justice's men made camp inside the mountain ring.

For three days Ember perched high on the mountain slope and watched the stalemate. Justice was capable of moving ahead and piercing further into Watergate, but only at the sacrifice of hundreds of soldiers on both sides. So, he had opted to hold his ground for the time. Ember waited in frustration.

As the evening shadows deepened during the third day, Ember heard a sound and looked down to see Dep making his way up the mountain.

What are you doing here? he asked.

Dep climbed the final reach, and sat down next to him, panting.

"I was looking for you," he said. "I am going to be leaving soon, but I wanted to say farewell first." He stopped to catch his breath. "You could've chosen an easier place to access though."

Ember smiled with amusement. *How did you get past the front lines?*

"Oh, Justice let me through. Tyrant has caught on to me and I need to get away; I barely made it out in time."

So now you are heading home?

Dep laughed. "Yes, I am. I've had quite enough of this whole business, so I'm going back to my castle now."

He stared out over the kingdom of Watergate. "I am going to miss you," he said.

And me you.

There was silence for a time, and then Dep said, "I do hope that this war is over quickly and that Tyrant gets what he deserves. He has always been a pain to the surrounding nations, but after what he's done now...to you and to Prosperity..." Dep trailed off for a moment, but then added angrily, "He does not deserve to live!"

I agree! His deeds are deserving of death; I wish that Peace would stop all this talk of mercy.

"I have heard that he offered to forgive Tyrant of everything, back in the palace."

He did! I was surprised with how soft he was with Tyrant. Even if the king had followed through, I still would not have trusted him. Treachery is in his nature.

"Aye, that is what he is—a traitor."

I wish that Peace would let me kill him.

"He doesn't want you to?"

No, neither me nor anyone else. Even now he wants Tyrant kept alive. I don't see why. Ember paused for a minute, and then added, *But Justice is here, so I suppose that whatever is decided will be what is right...even if it's not what I would've chosen.*

Dep nodded. "Well, I understand that. You must trust your Rider to do what is right."

Then suddenly, his voice was more urgent. "But if you do capture him, remember, Tyrant is a liar. He may pretend he wants peace but mark my words he will try to kill you the first chance he gets. Don't let him take you off guard!"

Ember nodded, and Dep got up.

"Good. I'm glad that I could see you one last time. I wish you good luck. Maybe you could come and visit me sometime, when this is all over; you know where I live, right?"

Yes, I do.

"Good, then may we meet again."

Yes, may we meet again.

***

Soon the sun disappeared completely behind the western mountains. Soldiers from both armies headed back to their tents for the night as darkness descended over the kingdom and as the cooler air enveloped the landscape with a gentle peace. But talks of war and battle plans were by no means quelled, and as the moon rose and night set in, Peace found Justice in his tent and spoke with him of a strategy he had in mind.

Justice listened carefully until Peace finished, and then he responded, "It is a good plan. In fact, I've wanted to do this ever since we advanced this far. But, of course, since it involved Ember and I was not the Rider, I could not suggest it. I am surprised however that *you* didn't think of this sooner."

"I always knew it was an option, but I never had any intention of carrying it out."

"Then why the change of mind now?"

"Because it was Ember who suggested it; and believe me, it took a lot of wearing down before I finally agreed."

"Before you agreed? Peace, this plan will allow us to end the war immediately with minimal bloodshed; why are you so hesitant to accept it? I would've done it in a heartbeat had I been you."

"I hesitate because it is dangerous."

"Are you afraid of getting hurt?"

"No. I'm afraid because it's dangerous to Ember."

Justice was surprised. "Dangerous to Ember? He's part of the Dragon Rider Pact. His life is filled with danger."

"But never before like this. There is a very real possibility that he could die in this mission."

"But if he suggested it to you, then he must be willing to take the risk."

"I knew from the beginning that he would; that is why I was careful not to suggest it."

"But why? If I were the Rider, I would've taken this course of action immediately."

Peace was silent for a moment; he seemed genuinely taken aback. Finally, he said, "Then perhaps this is why you were not made the Rider."

"What do you mean by that?"

"Tell me, would you have no concern for your dragon's life? Would you have been willing to possibly sacrifice him to end this war?"

"If there was indeed a good chance of ending the war, and if he were willing, then I would see no reason why not. Is that not what you swore to do? Wasn't it your oath to lead your dragon to do what was best for Tarenthia?"

"My oath was to do what was best first for *him*, and *then* for Tarenthia. As the Rider, it is my job to keep Ember from doing things that could be dangerous to himself, even things that he wants to do. I still don't feel good about this plan because of the danger it puts him in."

Justice waved his hand in a dismissive manner. "Fine, do as you will. But why do you come to me about this? If he is your dragon, then why tell me of your plan?"

"Because the very nature of this mission will prevent us from bringing many people—in fact, we can only carry two. I plan on going myself, but I will need someone else who has exceptional skill at hand-to-hand combat—naturally, that is you."

"Me? Why, Peace, I would be honored to fight alongside your dragon."

"So, you will come?"

"Certainly! I have one question though," Justice added.

"What?"

"Why is it that *you* are going? I respect that Ember is your dragon, but wouldn't your presence endanger the mission? What if you are captured again and they use you to subdue Ember? And furthermore, if you want experience with hand-to-hand combat, I have several men who—"

"I intend to go for two reasons. First, because Ember *is* my dragon and if he does die in this mission, I intend to die with him. But second, I want to be along to ensure that neither of you kills King Tyrant."

"What! Why? Why wouldn't you want him dead? Isn't that the whole point of this?"

"The whole point of this is to end the war. I intend to capture him and remove him from the throne, yes, but I do not want him harmed either now or after this is all over."

"Why? He has rebelled against the rule of Highland and even now resists us. He deserves death; and if you don't agree I'd think that Ember does."

"He does, and it took a lot of me wearing *him* down before he agreed not to harm Tyrant. But I still hold to preserving the king's life—it is of strategic importance to us. Think about it. How many of the soldiers that we are fighting against, do you think, *want* to be fighting the armies of Highland and the Dragon Rider?"

"Probably none of them."

"Then why do they do so?"

"Because they are loyal to their king."

"Yes! They do not like what their king demands, and many of them may even wish him dethroned and replaced, but all will fight to the end because they are his subjects. If we show them we have no intention of hurting Tyrant, how many of them might stop fighting us? How many might actually *approve* of our idea of replacing him?"

"Well, they're not going to seize him and send him out on a silver platter."

"No, not at all! But how many of them might turn a blind eye to us if they know what we are doing? How many would actually resist if they knew we are only trying to replace their king and not kill him? We could possibly end this war without losing another life."

Justice thought for a long while. Finally, he said, "I see your point, and I do agree that promising to keep Tyrant alive could be beneficial. I despise it though when people defy our father and get away with it; it burns within me when they face no penalty for their actions. However, you are the Dragon Rider; this mission belongs to you and if you desire that Tyrant be kept alive, then I will fight under your command."

"Thank you, Justice."

***

Early the next morning the air was crisp and cold, and as the sun had not yet made its way over the eastern mountains, it was dark as well. Many soldiers still slept; only the generals and night guards were awake. Few of them saw Ember crouched in the shadow of the mountain above the waterfall, and fewer still, having noticed, would've seen Peace and Justice standing by his side. A gentle tranquility rested across the kingdom despite what was soon to commence.

Peace examined his sword one more time in the dim light before sheathing it. It was a borrowed sword, his old one having been left behind during the escape; he hoped he would get it back soon. He looked up at the sky of dimming stars and mounted Ember who stood waiting impatiently. The dragon sniffed the air, surveyed the kingdom below, and let his eyes fall upon the castle, which stood stark and straight at the far end of the city.

When he felt Peace secure on his back, he said, *This might've worked better had we waited until further on in the day. Now we will be heading directly into the rising sun.*

True, said Peace, *but too many people would've seen us in the middle of the day, and there wouldn't have been enough light during the night. Fly quickly; maybe we'll make it before sunrise.*

Justice, wearing his traditional katana and dagger mounted and sat behind Peace. "Are we ready?" he asked.

"I believe so. Are your men ready to spread the message?"

"Yes, as soon as they see us leave, my messengers will tell the opposing army of our plans. It will be too late for them to stop us, but hopefully if they agree with what we are doing there will be no fighting while we are gone."

"Good," said Peace. And then to Ember, *Are you ready?*

The dragon crouched against the rocks his eyes focused.

Yes, I am eager to start.

Please be careful.

I will. Hold on!

And with that, Ember spread his wings and leapt from the mountainside. He flew hard, trying to gain altitude and speed. Below them Peace sensed shouts as they passed high over the heads of the Watergate army. He set his eyes forward. Far ahead of them, the castle loomed behind its walls crowned with skylances. Peace gulped and held tight to Ember's neck; Justice seemed delighted behind him. Between the peaks of the far mountains the sky lightened, making way for the approaching sun. Far ahead of them, near the castle, a horn sounded.

Keep going, Peace whispered. Ember flew harder.

Up ahead in the dim light, Peace made out two griffins as they leapt from the ground and began flying toward them. Ember noticed but held his course, his wings pumping a steady beat. Soon the beasts were nearly level with him and approaching fast.

Look out! warned Peace, who was beginning to feel sick. But he sensed from Ember an excitement, a glee, a type of bloodlust common to dragons.

We'll be fine, Ember said as the beat of his wings increased.

Try not to kill them if you can; they're only following the king's orders.

It may be impossible to reach the castle if I do not.

Then at least give them a warning.

Ember did so, sending out a threatening roar that echoed back across the mountains. Both griffins continued their attack. Behind him, Peace heard Justice laugh and yell out.

With the griffins nearly upon him, Ember turned his head and blasted fire, sending one screeching and tumbling down through the air, trailing smoke behind it like a phoenix. The other made a lunge at Ember's wing, but he swerved in an instant and caught the animal tightly in his claws. A minute later, it too was spinning toward the ground with its own wings torn.

"Here come more!" shouted Justice, and Ember looked up to see five this time, all heading toward him. He positioned himself to strike them with fire and waited for an opportune moment. But just then the rays of the rising sun shot out from behind the mountains and blinded his eyes. He breathed fire into the midst of them, but they all dodged in different directions and escaped unharmed.

"Look out!" cried Peace, and then they were all upon the dragon, hitting him from every angle. Ember immediately folded in his wings to protect them and plummeted in a dive toward the ground. He lashed out wildly with his tail and smacked one griffin squarely in the head, sending it spinning. On his back, Justice drew his sword and swung out, laughing, at the griffin clawing at the right wing. He hit it in the head and knocked it off, killing it.

Ember turned and shot fire toward the griffin at his left wing, searing it until it let go. With both of them now free, Ember snapped his wings open and swooped painfully out of his dive, trying to gain altitude again.

The last two griffins dove at him from above, one attempting to go over him and the other under. He directed his course toward the one trying to fly under and caught him squarely in his claws. The other flew over his head, but Justice jumped up from his back and slashed out with his sword, slicing the griffin across the belly, sending it spiraling. Ember released the griffin he held and leveled out. If there were any more of the creatures still alive, they did not attack again.

"Not bad," said Justice, sheathing his bloody sword.

Peace was aghast. "If you had a dragon of your own," he said, "half of Tarenthia could be destroyed in a day!"

Justice said nothing. It was obvious that he was enjoying the flight.

Ember was now approaching the castle's outer wall, and Peace could see the giant crossbows aimed up at them. *Please be careful!* he begged, but Ember seemed more excited than ever. The skylances began to fire and one by one Ember dodged the bolts.

The fools! The dragon scoffed. *They are all firing too early, leaving us time to evade them.*

Not all of them have fired though; be careful.

Stop worrying about me. I would enjoy doing this sort of thing more often.

You and your excitement! thought Peace.

They flew in close to the wall and several more of the skylances fired.

Interestingly enough, however, they missed by more than the ones that had fired sooner, for it is more difficult to keep a crossbow aimed ahead of a dragon when it is passing over than when it is far away. Ember flew by them all without incident.

Ahead of them stood the castle, and Ember dove for the giant court-yard right outside its gate. Two more skylances fired up at him from the ground, but he dodged them rolling first left, then right, landing power-fully upon the flagstones in triumph.

Caught up in the moment, he proceeded to blast fire in a circle all around himself, as though claiming his ground. Justice immediately leapt down from his back, and Peace followed on shaky legs. The soldiers who had moments ago been stationed in the courtyard were now fleeing for their lives.

Justice smiled at their hasty retreat. "Well done Ember! Well done! We've *got* to do that again sometime!"

"Are you serious!" cried Peace, trying to catch his breath.

Justice ran over to the heavy portcullis that had been lowered to block the entrance into the castle. He shook it uselessly, and then called out "Hey Ember, I could use your help with this."

The dragon lumbered over to the archway, barely big enough for him to fit through had it been open, and smashed his head against the gate. It shook and bent slightly, but otherwise held firm. Ember snorted, took a step back, and blasted fire at it for several seconds. Then he charged again, caught the softened metal frame in his horns, and wrenched it from its place, throwing it aside.

Justice hurried through the opening, pausing a moment to say thanks. Peace stayed behind a moment longer and stroked the dragon's neck.

We won't be long, he said. *Guard the entrance for us.*

I will; come back safely, my Eldar.

My Eldar, Peace agreed. Then he turned and hurried after Justice.

***

Together the brothers found a staircase and ascended it. Under most circumstances it would've been foolish for two ordinary swordsmen to try and storm a castle by themselves; but most of the guards were at the front lines and Justice was no ordinary swordsman.

At the top of the steps, they came across a great hall, perhaps used in times past for great feasts. At the far end, several steps led up to a pair of great doors and stationed on the steps stood eight soldiers. They immediately raised their weapons when they saw the intruders, but Justice only laughed and drew his sword and dagger.

Peace ran to his brother's side and engaged the first soldier he encountered. Justice charged past him and dispatched one of the men almost immediately with a block and a thrust. Two more attacked, but his two blades flashed and sent both men flying down the steps. Peace slew his man and stepped back to watch.

His brother fought with lightning speed, blocking a sword with his dagger, sweeping out with his katana, spinning left, then ducking right, and enjoying it all the while. In only a few seconds he had either disarmed or killed the other five, and stood at the top of the steps, daring others to come.

"You've gotten better than last I saw you," remarked Peace.

"I've had three years to practice. Look out behind you!"

Peace turned and saw a much larger group of men running in from the other end of the hall, many with crossbows. He looked at his sword for a minute, but then put it down and raised his hands to the approaching mob.

"Stop! We mean you no harm," he called out.

The soldiers slowed to a stop, but several pointed their swords at Peace's throat.

"What do you mean no harm? Look at what you've done here!" yelled one of them.

"We fight only those who attack us," said Justice, slowly descending the steps. Several crossbows were pointed at him.

"It is not our goal to kill anyone," said Peace. "We have nothing against you, your comrades, or your kingdom. We do not intend to hurt your king, but only to remove him from the throne in order to elect a more stable ruler."

The men started to protest, but Peace quickly continued, "We do this only because we desire what is best both for you and for Watergate. Tyrant has declared war on Highland, and you will all die if you continue to fight us. But we do not desire to fight you; let us remove him from the throne and by doing so heal Watergate of its oppression!

"We will not kill him; we will not hurt him; we mean only to take him back to our camp to reason with him. He will be returned to you, I promise. Your loyalty is to your king, but if you see that what he is doing is wrong, then please allow us to save him from himself."

The soldiers were silent for a moment, and then began to murmur amongst themselves. Finally, one of them stepped back and lowered his sword. He said, "If that truly is your purpose, to save our king and not to kill him, then I do not choose to stand in your way."

Several of the other soldiers grumbled and muttered, but they too stepped back. Peace was relieved.

"Can you tell me where we might find him?" he asked.

The soldier looked around him at his comrades, and then said, "You will find Tyrant on the uppermost floor. Take the steps there."

"Thank you, thank you so much," said Peace, picking up his sword. "Highland will remember and reward you for this."

Then he turned and, along with Justice, began to climb the stairs toward the top floor.

"You see," said Peace to Justice behind him. "Diplomacy is far more effective than the sword."

"Aye," said Justice, "...but only when diplomacy works."

It took several minutes to reach the top. Surprisingly, they didn't meet any guards along the way. Peace wondered if perhaps it was due to the fact that he and Justice had moved so quickly—there had not been enough time for any alarms to spread. When they got to the top, however, he realized that was not the reason at all.

Tyrant was expecting them.

The king stood in the center of the chamber at the top of the steps, and all around him were stationed his personal guards. Nearly a dozen crossbowmen stood in the back, aiming their weapons at the doorway.

Peace immediately dropped his sword and raised his hands when he entered the room. Justice did not.

Upon seeing them, Tyrant let out a sinister laugh and exclaimed, "So here you are Rider! You just couldn't get enough of me, could you? Did you really think that I would just let you walk in here and kill me? Ah, and you brought your brother as well; how pleasant! I do believe that now we will be able to turn this war around and finally—"

"We are not here to kill you," interrupted Peace, his voice calm, clear, and bold. "We are here to take you prisoner."

For just a second Tyrant lost his nerve and looked around in panic. Upon seeing all his men however, he seemed to regain his confidence. "You? Take me prisoner? Ha! I'd like to see you try."

"Tyrant, please, let's not let things get messy. Surrender yourself to us and we will all leave without any more bloodshed."

"But why would I ever surrender to you?"

"Because if you don't, we may have to insist."

"Insist? What do you mean?"

In answer, Peace touched the Link around his neck.

Suddenly there was a loud crash above them and the roof shook, cracks forming in the stone.

"Get them!" cried Tyrant wildly, and several of his men rushed toward Peace. Justice moved quickly in front of him.

There was another loud crash and this time a large section of the roof behind Tyrant collapsed and fell in with a cloud of dust and stone—and out from that cloud emerged Ember! Several crossbowmen fired uselessly at the dragon before dropping their weapons and running.

In the moments of confusion, Justice charged the king with Peace right behind him. Several guards tried to block his way, but he disarmed and knocked them aside with hardly a second glance.

With the Rider in front of him and the dragon behind, Tyrant held up his hands and screeched, "Stop! Please, I'll go with you. I surrender!"

Many of the guards were already fleeing, but the rest put down their weapons and backed away slowly. Justice quickly grabbed the king by the wrist and heaved him up onto Ember's back with Peace's help. Once he was secure, and when they had both mounted, Ember leapt through the hole in the roof and was gone.

***

Their flight back to camp was swift and uneventful—apparently soldiers are unwilling to shoot down a dragon who carries their king—and once Tyrant was in the custody of the Highland army, all the people of Watergate surrendered (and most quite willingly). Justice quickly took the opportunity to station his men throughout the city and suppress any ideas of surprise rebellion, but there seemed little chance of that now. Indeed, many of the citizens cheered when they saw Peace travel down the road with his army, almost as though a great cloud of fear and oppression had been lifted by his presence.

Tyrant was surprisingly cooperative. Ember was still suspicious of him, especially in light of the way he had acted before, but he also knew how cowardly the king was and that without any hidden daggers he wasn't likely to try anything foolish.

Tyrant almost seemed relieved that he'd been captured; over and over again he explained to Peace how he had never meant most of the things he had done, and how he was only acting out of obedience to a strange man and his band of followers. Peace questioned him about these men, but Tyrant only said that most of them had snuck off as the war started, and that he knew neither who they were nor where they had gone.

The celebration of the city's capture (celebrated by both the soldiers and the citizens) lasted for nearly two days. During that time, Peace attempted to arrange for a new king to take the throne—one who would treat his people fairly and honor their allegiance to Highland. Tyrant seemed disappointed at first, but he held no ill will and even offered to bring a spectacular end to the festivities by personally handing over to Peace the stolen emerald which had started the whole ordeal. Peace quickly agreed, seeing that many of the people still respected Tyrant and that Tyrant was eager to do something to make up for the way he had acted toward Highland.

The ceremonious transfer of the emerald was held at evening in the courtyard of the castle itself. Peace and Tyrant stood together in the center with Ember close by and a great crowd of people around the three of them. Justice was absent from the proceedings, ensuring order elsewhere in the kingdom. When everything was in place, Tyrant had his men bring the emerald in a giant treasure chest to the courtyard, where he unlocked it and prepared to open it. Before he did so however, he gave a speech to the great crowd around him.

"My good people!" he said. "Today is indeed a day to rejoice, for today our kingdom bears the honor of having the very Dragon Rider himself, along with Justice his brother, as our delighted guests! Before, I treated them poorly; but now I recognize that they never meant to harm any of us, but only desired our good and prosperity. Therefore today, as a token of my gratitude, I will present to the Rider the great emerald of Watergate. I know that it means much to us, and that it has been our pride for over one hundred years, but I see fit today to give such a token to the one who has brought us peace."

All around him, the people cheered as Tyrant finished his words and opened the chest.

"Today marks the beginning of a new era," he said, reaching inside for the emerald. "Like a new chapter of a book, today will become the start of a whole new age, free from oppression and foolish choices. Today, there will be a new order!"

The people cheered and Tyrant smiled.

"To the new order!" he called out.

"To the new order!" shouted the people, five of them particularly loudly.

Tyrant turned his eyes back to the chest, his smile now turned sinister. He drew forth the contents, holding it up in the setting sun for all to see. It was a blue dagger.

"And death to the Rider!"

In a moment too quick to fathom, Tyrant charged toward the dragon and five men at the front of the crowd drew hidden swords. Out of the corner of his eye Ember saw them raise their weapons and rush for Peace, but his attention was drawn entirely to the man with the poisoned dagger charging at him. At the same time Ember felt betrayal, hurt, and anger. He remembered Tyrant before, when he had stabbed him with a red dagger that burned him with fire, and he saw now the same man running at him again, this time with the intent to kill. With a sickening feeling he remembered Dep's warning, how Tyrant could not be trusted, and suddenly all he felt was anger and rage. He felt a boiling hatred for the man before him who was a traitor, a liar, and a murderer all at once;

and in that moment, his fury overtook him. He opened his mouth and charred the flagstones until they were black.

The men who were charging Peace saw the flame and stopped dead in their tracks in shock. The king was no more! All stood dumbfounded, unable to understand what had happened.

A moment later the attackers were in the custody of Justice's men and being hauled away. But Peace did not notice. He looked in horror at the blackened mark on the ground and then to Ember; his face showed an anger unlike any he had ever held before.

"Why did you do that?" he shouted out loud and in rage, his voice quivering. "Why did you kill him?"

Ember was taken aback. *He attacked me!*

"You didn't have to kill him!" Peace hollered. Around them, the crowd was dissolving into chaos with people shouting and yelling; Justice's men were moving in to restore order. "I promised that he would be kept alive! I gave them my word!"

He was going to kill me; how could you side with him? He betrayed us twice!

"I wanted him to change! I wanted a peaceful transfer of power, and now in one moment you have turned our victory into defeat!"

He attacked me! I've done nothing wrong. He deserved to die!

"You wanted him dead! You wanted to kill him from the beginning and you just couldn't control yourself!" Peace was walking toward him now; he had even drawn his sword in his rage. "Why couldn't you listen to me? Why did you prove me a liar in front of the whole kingdom?"

He deserved death! Everyone, except you, can see that! I should have killed him before, but you wouldn't let me. You're weak and incapable of justice!

Peace stabbed his sword into the ground between the stones. "And you are too violent! All you want is to kill and destroy. That's all you are, an irrational, murdering beast! An animal!"

Ember was taken aback. He stared at Peace in disbelief. His eyes revealed hurt. Then he turned, and with a power that shook the ground tore off into the skies, wings beating furiously as he headed for the mountains. Peace turned his back and headed in the opposite direction.

***

There were more soldiers than civilians in the courtyard by the time Justice arrived. He looked left, then right, bewildered by what had happened. He stepped forward to the blackened flagstones and tried to take in the situation.

"Was the dagger poisoned?"

Justice turned in surprise. The question had come from one of the five men who had attacked Peace. He was struggling against a soldier who was taking him away.

Justice motioned for the guard to stop, and then asked, "What did you say?"

"Was the dagger that Tyrant used actually poisoned?" repeated the man.

Justice looked at him oddly, but then picked up the blackened dagger from the flagstones.

"It has a hollow blade," explained the man. "It was supposed to be filled with poison, and if you push in the hilt it should come out the tip."

Justice looked at the dagger curiously and then said, "Why? Shouldn't it have been poisoned?"

"Well yes, it should've. But I wondered..."

"You wondered what?"

"Well...it's just a little suspicious. You see, there were eight of us at first; we all followed a leader. He formed an allegiance with Tyrant and helped arrange the trap for the Dragon Rider. But when the trap failed and three of us were captured, he came up with a new plan.

"He told us that he had put a poisoned dagger in the emerald chest, and that if Tyrant was ever captured we should all play along and pretend to hand over the emerald. Tyrant was to take the dagger and kill the dragon while the rest of us ran in and took Peace captive, which would've given us enough leverage to get away.

"Of course, none of that matters now; but I just wondered...he never actually let us see the dagger. Would it have worked? Did we really come so close to destroying the Dragon Rider?"

Justice stared at the man for a minute, then turned his eyes toward the dagger and pushed in the hilt.

"It's empty."

The man's eyes widened, then he yelled and struck the ground with his foot hollering, "He tricked us! He betrayed us! He promised us a kingdom, but he was only *using* us! We were duped; deceived!"

"Who was using you?"

"Our leader! He was always secretive; never letting us know more of his plan than necessary, hiding in the shadows, never telling us his real name..."

"Tell me where this man is, and I will find him! Is he here, in Watergate?"

"Watergate? No! He left! He told us the plan and then disappeared; I still don't know how."

"What do you know about him? Tell me—anything!"

"He was a crafty man who went by the name of Dep."

5

The Trap

It was dark and cold and damp. Ember stood stiffly in the room, listening to the drip, drip, drip from the ceiling. His body was frozen, but his mind was at war. There were too many feelings, too many emotions, surging through him at once. He bore the combined effect of them all but felt pangs of each individually as they swirled around. Anger, regret, loneliness, pain, pleasure.

No! He must not think of pleasure. He was ashamed of it, but it seemed beyond his control. A desire, a hunger, a longing for something he could not name.

Stop! Think of something else! He tried desperately to recreate the other feelings—the hurt, the loneliness, the awful emptiness. He felt the pain of them all and how they bore down on his soul—but at least they were natural. At least they were still part of who he was.

The agony was almost more than he could bear, but he pressed on, forcing himself to remember what had brought him here, reliving the heartbreaking past in sharp detail. Maybe he could reclaim himself.

Maybe Peace (the name still caused him to shudder), maybe he would come back. He had to hold on...

***

Two weeks earlier, Peace spent three days of continuous feverish work to lower the tensions in Watergate. After Tyrant had been killed there was almost a full-scale rebellion among the citizens who, while they did not necessarily agree with everything their king did, had admired him nonetheless. It was only by Justice's ever-present display of military force and Peace's consistent negotiating that war did not break out all over again.

Peace, after two tireless nights, had calmed the situation by convincing Prosperity to renounce their claim on the emerald (which they did reluctantly, but willingly). Peace then organized a proper burial for Tyrant and installed his son up as the next king. He did everything quickly and efficiently, but also ruthlessly, as if fueled by anger.

Justice did little during that time. He organized troops where Peace needed them, but for the most part he was lost deep in thought. He couldn't seem to get over the failed plot against Ember's life. What was its purpose? Why design a scheme to fail? What was there to be gained?

He puzzled over it long and hard, but then on the third day he realized something that he hadn't thought of before and quickly sought out Peace, requesting several hours alone with him.

"What do you want?" Peace asked him when they had ridden beyond the city gate.

"For starters, I think you're working too hard," said Justice.

"Keeping peace among these people requires my constant work. Especially in light of what happened three days ago."

"Yes, I understand, but don't you think that maybe you've been so caught up in fixing everything that you've neglected some of your greater duties?"

"Like what?" retorted Peace.

"Like Ember. He's been gone three days, and no one has seen any sign of him."

"So? If he chooses to get mad and fly off for a while, what is that to me?"

"Because he is your dragon; you should be concerned about his welfare," said Justice.

"He's fine; I have other things to worry about."

"No, you don't—and I think you are trying to avoid the problem by burying yourself in your work."

"I'm not avoiding anything. Ember will come back once he has calmed down."

Justice was silent for a moment. After a little, he turned and said, "Tell me, why do you think Ember left?"

"Because he was angry. He wanted to kill Tyrant and blames my mercy for all this trouble."

"Is that really what you think?"

"Yes, why?"

"Because I think he left because he was heartbroken."

Peace turned to him angrily. "Heartbroken? You know nothing about heartbreak! And you know nothing about Ember either! What gives you the right to lecture me on my own dragon?"

Justice was silent for another moment, and then said, "It is true that I know little about heartbreak for I have never experienced it, and it is also true that I know little about Ember for he was never my dragon. But I *do* know about anger—and believe me when I say that no amount of rage would've kept any Rider's dragon away for three days. Anger burns like fire; it can lead people to do rash things, and it can damage the relationship between even the best of friends. But like any flame, anger eventually burns down—and when it does, it will be replaced with either a great bitterness for the other person, or a desire to resolve the problem. Ember would have been back by now had he only been angry."

Peace was incredulous. "You believe that he left because he thought that I rejected him?"

"Your exchange was fierce. He may have taken it to heart more than you realize."

"That's ridiculous! How could you possibly think that I, as the Rider, would reject my own dragon? He's certainly headstrong and impulsive at times, but that does not mean that I would disown him. How dare you accuse me of doing something like that to the thing I treasure most, to the gem of my heart. You know that I would never do that!"

"Of course I know that," said Justice, his voice kind but grave. "But does Ember?"

＊

Ember had left Watergate, his wings beating furiously, his vision blinded by tears. As he soared toward the tips of the mountains with great speed, he was aware only of a heavy force which seemed to drive him away—away from Watergate, away from the remains of Tyrant, away from Peace. He understood little else as he tore through the sky, the wind whistling past him as he flew faster than he ever had before. Never had he felt such a murderous mixture of pain, rage, and loss.

Peace had called him an animal, and so like an animal Ember wandered the plains of Tarenthia for a day and a half. He flew through the clouds, hunted for food, and drank from water holes alone—always alone. All the other beasts and birds fled from his presence and it occurred to him for the first time how much he was shunned by all else. No animal wanted to be anywhere near a dragon, and men would not welcome one either. In fact, the only one who had actually wanted to be around him, who had ever loved him, was Peace. And now Peace despised him.

Ember felt great anger within himself, but he couldn't target it toward anyone in particular. Sometimes he hated Peace for not wanting him to kill the king, but he could not bring himself to hate his Rider. Sometimes he was angry at himself for what he had done, but he could not feel that way for long because he still believed that he acted justly.

Ember shook his head and stared at his own reflection in the water as he drank. He wished it had never happened. Oh, what wouldn't he give to reverse that moment? Never before had he felt so alone, so empty, so despised. Why had he done it? Why hadn't he just stopped and thought things through? It all happened so fast; Tyrant charging toward him with the dagger, and Dep's warning that he would do so echoing in his mind...

Dep.

Ember stopped short. Dep had warned him that it would happen. How could he have known? It didn't seem odd at the time, but now upon reflection Ember realized that the way Dep told him about Tyrant's betrayal had been different than the way he'd said everything else. It hadn't been a warning; it had been a foretelling.

Ember quickly retraced the rest of the conversation on the mountain. Dep claimed that he had come to say farewell, but the majority of their discussion had focused on Tyrant and how he deserved death. It was almost as if Dep had wanted him to hate the king, wanted him to be on edge, wanted him to react, in the event that...

Ember was in the skies now, his eyes scanning the horizon to the east, the direction where Dep had said his castle lay. The more he thought about it, the more suspicious he became.

Dep was always showing up at just the right time, overhearing just the necessary things; was it possible that a single ambassador could be so lucky as to show up at Prosperity in time to both overhear the plot and to warn him? Was it possible that such an ambassador would also have both the knowledge and skill to find a dragon dungeon and break into it? How had he guessed so quickly the description of the man in the courtyard? How did he escape so easily from Tyrant at the start of the war? How did he know so much? How could he have known?

Ember's wings were beating furiously and his rage returned stronger than before. Had he been under a more rational mindset, he might've stopped and considered that maybe he was jumping to conclusions, that he didn't have enough information to cast any blame—that despite acting suspiciously, Dep had also been the one to release him from prison and warned him on the mountain to follow his Rider. But Ember thought of none of those things. His anger had finally found a target, found someone to blame, and he was not about to let it go. Dep would pay for what he had done to him!

∗∗∗

Peace thought for several minutes, mulling over what Justice had said. He hadn't considered that Ember would actually think himself rejected. But then again, the dragon had been gone for a while.

"If he doesn't return by tomorrow, then perhaps we should organize a search party to find him," said Peace hesitantly.

"No," said Justice, his voice becoming a bit more urgent. "I think we should go now. Ember could be in great danger."

"Danger? You're the one who wanted him to attack an enemy castle surrounded by skylances. You didn't seem very concerned about his safety then."

"I wasn't concerned at that time because that was an expected danger."

"Expected?"

"When the Dragon Riders were first created, it was expected that they would experience danger. We all knew that as you fought for peace among the kingdoms some would try to kill you. But it was all *anticipated* danger; the King knew you would encounter it, and he also knew that you were equipped to deal with it. This here though, this was never supposed to happen. This is a danger that neither you nor Ember were ever prepared to deal with."

"What danger? Ember is a dragon; he can take care of himself. What is there to be afraid of?"

"Tell me, have you ever heard of a man named Dep?"

Peace was surprised. "Dep? Why yes, Ember told me a bit about him. He helped us escape from Watergate."

"And have you heard that he was the one behind Tyrant's rash attempt on Ember's life?"

"Well yes, I've heard bits and pieces. But I don't believe any of it. Whoever set this whole thing up was angry that Dep ruined his trap, and so his last act was naturally to try and throw suspicion on him."

"Tell me; have you ever actually seen Dep in person?"

"Only for a few minutes; he stopped to tell me that it would be of strategic importance to keep Tyrant alive."

"Interesting...I saw him briefly too when he was fleeing Watergate to our side. He told me where Tyrant was hiding and suggested that we fly in and try to capture him. But there was something that made me suspicious about him."

"Why? If that is what he told you, then isn't it obvious he wasn't working with Tyrant? Have you heard of this Dep before?"

Justice was silent a moment.

Finally, he said, "No, I have never heard of anyone called Dep. But just this morning, I realized that I *have* read of someone whose name could be shortened to Dep—someone who once committed a great crime against Highland."

"That's hardly enough information to convict him. You could be overreacting."

"I wish I were...and let us hope for Ember's sake that I am. But you are forgetting something very important."

"And what is that?"

"A Link. Dep would've needed one to talk to Ember."

"Yes, but what's so wrong with that? He told Ember—Highland gave him one as a token of thanks for helping our father years ago."

Justice looked at him incredulously. "Did you pay no attention to any schoolbook that didn't talk about dragons? Your command of history and law are about as bad as your command of fencing. *Highland has never given a Link to a commoner!* The Links are seen as sacred—worthy of being worn only by a Dragon Rider and his dragon."

"But then, where else could he have gotten the Link?"

"While Highland has never given one away willfully, there is a record of someone who once took a Link by force. If he has that Link, then there is no other person Dep could be, for it was a crime that has only been committed once."

Peace was taken aback and looked at Justice in surprise.

"Tell me, what was this man's full name?"

***

Evening was setting in when Ember spotted the clearing in the forest from overhead. He was still several miles from Dep's castle, which he could see in the distance near the eastern shore, but the rare break in the woods had caught his eye. The trees had all been so tall and grown so close together that the clearing proved to be the first place where he was capable of landing for quite some time. He could've made it to the castle if he had wanted to, but upon seeing the opening below his plans changed, for in it he saw a small group of people—one of whom was standing off by himself in the center.

Ember folded his wings and dove. The loneliness and the pain within him still throbbed, but his wrath now burned with full force. He hit the ground with the might of an earthquake—a landing of such power and rage that it surpassed anything he had ever done before. Most of the men stood at the opposite end of the clearing and beside them there was a large empty wagon that could've held ten horses. But Ember hardly glanced at them, for his attention was drawn to the man who stood in front, alone, in the center of the clearing.

Dep.

Dep took several steps forward good-naturedly. He wore his saber at his side, but aside from that he was without weapon, armor, or shield.

"Ember! My good friend! How nice to see you again! I'm surprised that you made it out here so soon. Tell me, what brings you here?"

Ember was undeterred. He spoke coldly, and angrily. *Why did you make me kill Tyrant?*

Dep looked surprised. "Me? What could I have done? I've been here all this time."

Don't play games with me! Ember roared. *You knew about the plot—you knew it would happen!*

Dep stopped short at the dragon's persistence, but then smiled. "You are a smart one, aren't you? I can see that you are not fooled. So, did you finally catch on? Did you realize what I had been doing?"

Yes, I did, and now you will pay for it!

Dep seemed saddened. "So, you're here to kill me?"

Yes.

Dep nodded. He slowly drew his saber with his right hand. "How ironic," he said, "that I should be killed by the very creature that I love most. But I suppose that is the fate I deserve."

He stabbed his saber into the ground next to him, and took several steps forward, leaving it behind. "Ember, please, before you kill me, I ask one thing. Let me tell you why I did what I did. It really was all for your own good; I ensured that the dagger wasn't poisoned."

But why? How much of our troubles at Watergate came from your own hand?

"Everything that happened at Watergate was from my hand. I played both sides—and that was very clever of me to do—because then I would have complete control." Dep looked upwards and smiled briefly to himself in a sad sort of way. "I had the perfect plan, and I was immune from detection on both sides...until now."

What plan? What were you trying to do?

Dep looked at Ember and grinned. "Ah, my plan! You'll be the first one to hear it, you know. I really do want you to know about it—I wanted so badly to tell you when I rescued you from that dungeon. But of course, if I had told my plan *then,* it would've defeated the purpose of my *having* the plan in the first place."

What plan? Tell me! And Ember snorted smoke just to make his point perfectly clear.

Dep nodded. "Aye, I will tell you. But if we are going to finally talk about my scheme, then I think it's time you knew me by my real name."

I thought it was Dep.

"No. It is Deception."

***

"Deception was once a servant in the royal household of Highland," said Justice, recollecting what he could from his history books. "He actually used to be a peasant boy, abandoned by his family and left to die on the streets. But the King of Highland at that time, our grandfather, took pity on him and brought him to the castle where he fed him, housed him, and made him a servant of his son, our father."

"And Deception did not like this?"

"No! Quite on the contrary, it was the happiest time of Deception's life, though that was not his name at the time. He was very similar to you in that he had an undying love for dragons. Being in the royal household gave him access to education about them, and on very few occasions he was even permitted to see the actual dragon eggs. It was the boy's dream come true!

"Unfortunately, however, it wasn't enough. The more Deception learned about dragons, the more he wanted one of his own. For years he thought that if he just worked hard enough, then perhaps one day the King might grant him a dragon. Apparently, he did not understand that the dragons are only ever given to the one named the Dragon Rider, and the Dragon Rider is always one of royal blood. When the day came for our father to receive his dragon, and when Deception began to learn, or perhaps finally admit to himself, that he was not about to have one, he grew envious."

"Why did our grandfather never give him a dragon?" asked Peace, rather concerned. "It seems like such a small favor to grant."

"Aye, it might've seemed that way at the time. But it would've gone against all the traditions that have led our country for over two millennia. But even in the face of that, our grandfather still considered giving him one."

"Then why didn't he?"

"Because Deception didn't actually love dragons...at least, not like he should have. Rather, he saw them as a source of power, as the ultimate freedom for himself. In the end it was decided that, while Deception craved dragons in a way that no king ever had, he could never actually *love* one. He was obsessed with them but cared only for how they made him feel and for what they could give him rather than for how he could love one. So, he was never given one—and he hated the King for it. Many days went by where he would gaze longingly at Glory, to the point where the young dragon began to fear him and hid from his presence. This of course, only affirmed our grandfather's decision."

"And so that was when he left?"

"Yes. He chose his date well, three days before the Sending Out, when all was busy in preparation for the celebration, and when it was most crucial that the King and the new Rider be present as the date approached. He changed his name to Deception, stole a Link from the treasure holds, and fled the castle. He was far away before anyone realized what had happened, and neither the King nor his son could do anything until the Sending Out was completed. Our father left as soon as he could and searched the countryside for Deception but never found him. Later that year there were reports that a man matching his description had drowned in quicksand, and Deception was believed to be dead."

"But you think he has come back?" said Peace. "You think that he faked his death and hid for all these years?"

"If he has, then we are all in grave danger."

"But how? Deception is one man; what danger does he pose to us or Highland?"

"He is deadly because of his hatred for the King. That is why I said he was an unexpected danger. It was expected that you would encounter men that hated other kingdoms, but this man hates Highland itself! If he really has been alive all these years, then that means he has had much time to plan his revenge—and he would only come out of hiding if he were certain that he had a plan that would work."

"But his plan failed! He tried to capture us and we escaped, and then he tried to kill Ember through Tyrant and that also did not succeed."

"But he was also the one responsible for getting Ember out of the dungeon in the first place, and the dagger he gave to Tyrant was never poisoned."

"But that makes no sense! What could he have achieved by that?"

"Perhaps instead of trying to guess what he wanted to achieve, maybe we should take a closer look at what he *did* achieve."

"Which was what?"

"He created an argument between you and Ember that separated the two of you from each other, and now Ember is flying without a Rider somewhere out in the wilds of Tarenthia!"

"But what could he gain from that? If anything, I am Ember's restraining force; if he were to find out what Deception had done, that man would most certainly die!"

"But Deception is a master schemer...one of the greatest ever known. Tell me, do you know where he lives—that is, where his castle is located?"

"Yes, it's three days east of here by the sea."

"And how did you know that?"

"Because Ember told me."

"That is exactly what I feared; Ember is certainly in grave danger now."

"How do you know?"

"Tell me Peace, *if* your plan is to declare war on the Dragon Rider and to get the dragon to think that he has been rejected so that he roams the countryside angry and alone, *if* that is your plan, then what is the one thing you will *never* do if you value your life?"

"What?"

"You tell that dragon where you live."

Peace eyes widened. "So, you're saying that Deception *wants* Ember to find him? But that would be suicidal! Why?"

"His reason is not important. What's important is that he wants it, and that alone is enough to make me drag an army across the country to stop him."

Peace nodded nervously, his face pale. "Then we must go at once! Organize the army to move out. I'll see what I can do here to ensure war will not break out again while we're gone. We will ride out with a search party ahead of the troops; maybe we can find Ember before he finds Deception."

Justice nodded.

"Let us hope we can find him. Let us hope it is not too late."

***

Deception advanced closer to Ember—his movements slow and final, as though they would be his last. Ember stood crouched and ready to spring upon the man at any moment. He could hardly contain the fire within him as he listened to Deception's confession.

"You nearly *did* ruin my plan," he said. "That's really quite remarkable to think about; over a decade to plan everything and you almost ruined it. Fortunately, I was able to improvise, and through quick thinking I generated the argument with your Rider."

So, it was your design to make him hate me all along!

"Not necessarily all along, but yes, it was my doing. Before I left, I made sure to speak with everyone. I told Peace how important it was that he keep Tyrant alive; I told you how important it was that Tyrant be killed; I told Justice that the best way to end the war would be to try and capture the king; and I told Tyrant that in the event he was captured he should go through with my little assassination plan. Everything I said was designed to bring about one inevitable conclusion."

Ember's rage had reached its peak. He growled and prepared to spring. *You will die for this!*

Deception stopped suddenly and smiled. He was now standing directly in front of Ember. "You are angry," he said. "I can see that clearly. But I am not fooled by it. I see beyond your rage into what it is hiding. I am not deceived! I know you, I know your heart, and you are trembling inside. Your anger is only a cover-up for the pain that has racked you from the day that you were rejected by your Rider. You hate me dearly, but that is only because you cannot hate Peace. You still love him; deep down inside he is still the only thing you want. You long to see him again, to be reunited with him, to feel his touch!"

And then, with the swift movement of a snake, Deception leapt forward and placed his hand on Ember's forehead between his eyes.

Immediately, Ember felt a shock within him unlike anything he ever felt before. It was a craving, a longing, and a sword all at the same time. It overwhelmed his mind and pierced him to the very core of who he was. There was no escape from it, no way possible to shield himself from its stabbing. He could not understand; all at the same time it was pain and pleasure, joy and unspeakable agony, fire and hunger.

With a jolt of surprise, he leapt backward, away from the man's hand, landing hard in a defensive posture. Deception laughed wildly.

"It works!" he shouted. "It finally works!"

Ember shook his head and tried desperately to pull himself together. The feeling had disappeared the moment he leapt away, but it had left a searing hole in its place. What was it? What did it mean? He had felt nothing like it before; he couldn't even decide whether it was pleasurable or painful. But he knew he wanted it again—he had to find out what it was, where it came from. Was it a hunger? A longing? For what?

Somehow it seemed to bear with it the tint of undeniable importance, as though it were somehow connected to the ultimate goal of life—that if he could just figure out what it was and capture it, then he would experience absolute bliss. And yet its identity eluded him, drove him mad, made him wish to feel the hunger again so that he could search harder.

"I tried to do this before, you know," said Deception, slowly moving closer again. Ember tried to blast him with fire, but for some reason he couldn't—he couldn't *choose* to do it. The emotion was somehow wrapped up with the man, and if he was to ever to feel it again...

"The first time was outside Prosperity, when I met you and warned you of the trap," continued Deception. "I tried to touch you there, but you were so concerned with the welfare of your Rider that you didn't even notice. So, I tried again after you had rotted a while in my dungeon. That time you let me touch you, and I saw in your eyes that you derived comfort from me, but even then your concern for the safety of your Rider proved too strong to overcome. I saw then that separating the two of you by force would never work—that if I ever wanted to get through to you, I would have to get you to leave him *willingly*."

Ember shook his head, trying to understand but not hearing. The feeling confused him, consumed him.

"And so, I devised my little scheme," continued Deception. "I had to work quickly to pull something together so fast, but I did it. I found the one thing that the two of you would disagree over the most, and with the engine of a full-scale war behind me, I raised the stakes higher than Peace could handle. Naturally when the disagreement came, the exchange would be fierce and painful. It was bound to make you leave in anger—so much anger in fact that you would pay no regard to whom you were leaving behind."

Dep struck out again at Ember and once again the dragon was overwhelmed by the sudden feeling. It seemed so sad, so painful, like a mournful longing. It caused him to want something more than he ever had in his life; something he would've been willing to sacrifice everything to get! But as hard as he tried, he couldn't figure out what it was.

With the last of his strength, Ember pulled himself away from Deception's hand and sank to the ground, weak and whimpering; an inexpressible sadness was flooding his mind. Deception knelt next to him.

"Let me tell you a little secret," he said, his voice soft. "You're not a natural dragon."

Ember did not look up, and Deception continued. "You have been modified, genetically changed, just like every dragon before you. It's Highland's way of keeping control over your kind, and through you, the rest of the world.

"There was once a time—a very, very long time ago—when no kingdom was greater than any of the others. Highland was just another name on the map, fighting for control like every other nation. Of course, there were dragons at that time, but they were all free and wild, unconquerable and untamable. But then Highland discovered a way of controlling the dragons and used them to force every other civilization into submission.

"You see, they had discovered that a dragon egg submerged in cold water weakens the fire of the hatchling within. It became more docile, submissive, dependent. When the dragon hatched, it would never know what had happened to it, that the hunger inside to be ruled by a Rider was not natural to dragons. It would never know that it was now living in slavery, that the kingdom of Highland had broken its will.

"It's a pity, really. I hate it when I see a race forcibly enslaved, but when I see a race that was once proud and free and unconquerable, when I see it groveling at the feet of humans, craving subjugation, actually *wanting* to be controlled—that just makes me sick!"

Deception reached out his hand again, and Ember whimpered when he saw it. He could not bring himself to move farther away.

"You feel it within, don't you?" Deception said, holding his hand just a little away. "So long has Peace controlled you, that you don't understand how to live without him. You are desperate to be touched by him again; you long to hear his voice again; you need to feel his weight on your back again. Look at you! You're the most powerful beast in the world and all you want is to be controlled! You can't function by yourself; the weight of handling your own destiny is crushing you—you're desperate to trust in someone else for your welfare, to let them lead you, to make decisions for you—you long to give someone your very soul!"

He leaned in close to the dragon, and whispered, "Give it to me."

He laid his hand on Ember's forehead again, and the dragon trembled and whined beneath it. But Deception could see that the dragon no longer had the power to resist; its longing for a master had grown too great to ignore.

"Come with me," he said. "Come with me, and we will set right these terrible wrongs. Together, we can overthrow Highland with the very weapon they used against the nations. They've broken you so that you can no longer function on your own, but I can still lead you to do great things! Together we will set free the race of dragons, and they will once again become wild and unconquered by humans! The damage the King has done to you is irreversible, but among your own kind you will yet become a legend, the very means of their salvation! Join me, and we will end this reign of slavery forever!"

Beneath his hand, Ember continued to tremble, a part of him still trying to fight off the influence.

"Just give up," Deception said soothingly. "Give in to me—it will all be made right. I will not hurt you; I will not use you. I will protect you, and this longing that you have inside of you I will fill—I will give you all the desires of your heart. Don't be afraid; I promise that you will be safe in my hands. Trust me—I never lie."

Slowly, the dragon beneath his hand ceased trembling, and was still. Then it looked up into his eyes and began to purr. Deception smiled.

"Yes!" he shouted. "Yes! Now we shall work together to save the races of both dragon and man. The road may seem long and difficult before us, but I have a plan—and Highland will fall beneath it. But today we can celebrate, for while there is still much to do, we have won a great victory! A new order has come!"

Deception looked up, smiling in triumph. "And the Pact of the Dragon Rider has fallen!"

***

Three days later, Peace and Justice arrived at the clearing, but of course by then it was too late. They knew that Ember had landed there, for they saw his tracks, but what they could not understand was why he had apparently jumped backward at one point as though afraid, without any evidence of a fight.

It was Justice who eventually found the two sets of tracks left by the large cart—one set noticeably deeper than the other. They discussed what the cart might have carried to the clearing that was so heavy, and it was eventually concluded that the cart must've come empty and carried something heavy away.

And there was only one thing in that clearing that would've been heavy enough to leave such deep wheel ruts—a dragon. Peace was certain that it was impossible for Ember to have been captured, especially with no sign of any struggle.

But Justice said nothing, turning his eyes in the direction of the tracks that led toward the castle in the distance. Then he turned and rode back to his army.

***

Ember knew not how long he stood in the chamber listening to the *drip, drip, drip* from the ceiling before a new sound awoke him from his contemplation. He looked up, dreadful fear and joyful anticipation running through him at the same time. The door to the chamber opened and strong light spilled into the room. Deception stood in the doorway.

"Greetings, my dragon," he said.

Instantly, Ember felt himself almost leap with excitement—and he hated himself for it. What would Peace think if he could see him now? Maybe he would forgive him. He hoped that he would...he hoped that he would still want forgiveness...

Deception came forward to lay his hand on him, and Ember backed away reflexively. It was out of instinct that he shrank back; in reality, every fiber of his being was trembling with excitement, longing for the feeling that always came with the man's touch. He had decided that he did like it, even if it was only the hunger and not the thing itself. He wished he didn't like it, he wished that he could control the longing he had for the man, but he could not. Deception reached out and touched him, and instantly Ember was filled with pleasure.

"It is all right, don't be afraid. You are still unsettled, but soon that will pass."

He rubbed Ember's neck for a few moments in silence, then he whispered, "The armies of Highland have assembled outside our gates. Your old Rider will be among them."

Ember said nothing, choosing rather to bask in the bliss, the safety, and the comfort that came from the man's hand.

"They will try to take you from me," Deception said, looking up at the ceiling, letting his fingers run across the scales of the dragon. And he smiled.

"Oh Ember, whatever shall we do?"

6

The Victory

They were three days into the siege and Peace was restless. This was taking too long. Somewhere on the other side of the wall was Ember, and he was in the hands of Deception. Was he being starved? Tortured? Was he going to be killed? Peace pulled at his hair in frustration and watched helplessly as Justice continued issuing orders and commands to soldiers, telling some to go here and some to go there and others to help with the battering ram.

At first it appeared an easy fortress to invade. The stronghold had only a short stretch of outer wall that blockaded the gap between two mountains, and only a single gate within that wall. Behind the wall stood a keep and behind the keep there was only the great glittering expanse of the Eastern Sea. It was this location that had given the fortress its name—World's End.

Justice was surprised that Deception would have chosen such a small, scarcely fortified hideout to run to. True, the walls were thick, and the keep tall and formidable, but the setup was no castle. Even still, it was proving difficult to capture.

"If this is such a poorly fortified base, then why is this taking so long?" demanded Peace of his brother on the third day. "Deception is likely sitting up there in his tower laughing at our efforts!"

"Just because his stronghold is poorly fortified does not mean that it can be broken into quickly," replied Justice curtly. "If I had a dragon or siege tower, I would've been able to take this fort in under an hour. However, since both are beyond us, I must resort to slower means. We will still be able to break in, and the battering ram is making significant progress, but it will take time."

"But we don't *have* time! Deception has Ember right now and he could be doing anything to him. No doubt he has a plan, and every second that we fail to stop him is another second that he is outwitting us. How is it

that Deception is able to keep us out with a squad of no more than thirty soldiers? He is making a mockery of Highland's forces!"

"Listen, I have no idea what Deception is playing at, but when that gate falls it will be over for him. He has nowhere to run—the sea lies behind him, and he cannot travel far along the shore before coming to the mountains. I don't know what he is planning on doing, but he will not keep us out much longer; we will have him soon!"

"What if he's planning another trap...this one for us?"

"I think that he might be. I am concerned that Deception has chosen so few soldiers to guard this fortress. I'm sure that he must have more."

"Perhaps he intends for his men to come around behind us and attack our army from the rear."

"I have already planned for that. I've built barricades behind us and sent scouts to watch for enemy troops. If that is his plan, he will not take us by surprise."

"Good! Then perhaps we may have outwitted him."

"I would hope so...though I suspect that someone as cunning as Deception is not unprepared for me."

***

And so, the attack continued. Hour after hour the battering ram pounded against the iron gate that, despite the bulges and cracks appearing in it, was still holding firm. Justice continued to tirelessly command his men; he seemed undaunted, calm, determined, but Peace sensed behind all of it a hidden rage flowing through him. Justice could certainly be patient, but as he stood steadfast and cool watching the gate slowly give way to his ram, Peace could see that there was no power aside from God Himself that could save Deception from Justice's resolve once he finally got inside.

Peace, however, was not as patient. He paced the camp restlessly as the day wore on, agonized with thoughts of Ember. That dragon was his life, his love. If he were to be killed, Peace did not know how he could go on. And as the day faded to evening, his restlessness only grew greater and more unbearable.

Finally night came, and much of camp slept. All was quiet except for the continual *bam, bam, bam* of the ram, which Justice had ordered to continue its work at all hours of the day. Peace was unable to sleep, and so he wandered the camp, lost in his misery.

He realized that his steps slowly began to take him closer to the wall, drawing him nearer to where he knew his companion would be. Of course, it was dangerous—the soldiers on the wall, as few as there were, could easily kill him with a well-aimed arrow. But it was also the darkest part of the night, and as Peace drew closer, he did not worry for his safety. The night was calm and cool, which both comforted and mocked his lonely feelings at the same time.

Eventually he slumped to the ground, his back against the stone wall, and he whispered to himself, "Oh Ember, Ember; my Eldar. What have I done to you?"

And then suddenly he felt another conscience near his, one that seemed to be probing and searching for him. Peace quickly sat up and called through the Link, *Ember, are you there?*

Peace! Yes, it's me. Are you really here?

Yes, I am. Oh Ember, you're alive! Are you okay? Are you hurt?

No I'm...fine; I just need to see you again. You cannot believe how happy I am to hear you! I was afraid that you'd been killed in the attack—I thought we might never see each other again.

I was afraid of the same; thank goodness you're alive! Quick, tell me where you are!

Far underground somewhere. I have to press myself against the wall just to hear you.

You'll be all right; tell me where you are, and I'll find you.

I don't know exactly—it's a maze down here. It won't matter by tomorrow though; Deception is worried about the progress you are making. He's afraid you're going to break in soon, and so he's beginning the final part of his plan.

What do you mean?

I don't know. He's planning to leave, to take me with him—I don't know where. He said we'll be going someplace where you will never be able to get us. You have to hurry! You have to...he's coming!

Ember! Peace shouted, but he lost his grip on his consciousness, as though it were being dragged away from him.

He stood up and beat the wall angrily with his fists, calling for his dragon, but only the emptiness of night and the *bam, bam, bam* answered him. Then he looked up, gritted his teeth, and marched back to camp.

"Justice!" he said, when he found his brother awake, silently watching the progress against the gate.

"What is it?" he asked.

"We have to get in! We have to get in now!"

Justice spun upon him angrily. "What do you think I'm trying to do? My men are working as hard as they can."

"It's not enough, we're out of time! I talked to Ember; I went to the wall and through my Link I was able to reach him in a passage underground. He said Deception is leaving with him for some place that we won't be able to follow. We have to get in there now!"

"I'm doing everything I can!" growled Justice. "I want to break in as much as you do! My men can't go any faster!"

"Then we have to try something else."

"There is nothing else!" yelled Justice. "I've thought of everything—the ram is our only way in!"

Peace looked away and there was silence for a moment between them. Justice turned his gaze back to the wall, watching his men hammer at the gate. Then in a voice much softer than before, he said, "Did Ember say he was being held underground?"

"Yes, he did."

"And did he say anything about what it was like—such as whether he was in a naturally formed tunnel, or one dug by man?"

"I don't know. He didn't say anything about it—only that it was like a maze. Why should that matter?"

"Because if there really is a large network of tunnels down there, then perhaps they are partly natural. Maybe Deception found them and decided to put them to use."

Peace could sense excitement rising in Justice's voice, and he began to grow excited himself. "Then what does that mean for us? Why is that important?"

"Because if those caves are natural," said Justice, turning his eyes to the rocky mountains on either end of the fortress wall, "then they must have had a natural opening."

Then he hollered out, "I need a troop of ten men, and horses for them all. Get some lanterns too; we leave immediately!"

The soldiers around him quickly sprang into action as Justice made for his horse with Peace close behind him.

***

Despite the enormity of the mountain, their search was not in vain. When they arrived at the base, Justice had his men climb the rocks and look for any trace of a cave or tunnel opening. For nearly half an hour they found nothing, but then, as the shades of sunrise were slowly starting to appear in the East, one of the soldiers found a hole between the rocks that led down into darkness. When the others arrived, they lowered a lantern and found at the bottom the opening of a cave that seemed to head in the general direction of World's End. Justice was delighted.

"Two men take the horses back to camp. The rest of you, come with me." And then he made his way down into the depths with Peace close behind.

They had indeed found a cave, but as they followed it further and further down into the earth, it seemed to be without end. Peace became nervous when it turned several times and didn't seem to be heading in the right direction anymore.

Finally, he said to Justice, "Are you certain that this is the right cave? Will this lead into World's End?"

"It will," said Justice coldly, his eyes focused ahead of him.

"But what if this only leads to a dead end? Or what if this is a trap? Doesn't it seem odd that Deception chose a castle with a tunnel leading straight into it?"

"It's not strange at all. In fact, it's a bit of genius. A secret tunnel like this gives those inside an escape, out from behind the attacking army. It also provides the means for a sneak attack. As long as we didn't know about this tunnel, Deception could use it to his advantage."

"So, you think maybe we outwitted him?"

"Perhaps."

They continued further in silence. Justice's determination was finally rewarded when they found a passage with sand covering the floor. Traveling further down, they began to observe wooden supports against the walls which helped to hold up the ceiling.

Justice smirked. "See? We are going the right way."

Peace nodded and continued to follow him along with the other eight soldiers.

Their luck ran out, however, when they came across a large chamber with tunnels leading out from it in all directions. At the moment it seemed deserted.

"Which way?" asked one of the men, his voice echoing around them.

"Split up!" ordered Justice, and they did accordingly. Peace chose a passage at random and traveled down it for a while, his only company a lantern that cast strange shadows across the rocky walls and ceiling. Suddenly, Peace began to feel the presence of another consciousness—one that he knew well!

Quickly, he hurried down the cave calling out, *Ember! Ember!*

From what appeared to be a distance, he heard a faint reply. *Peace? Ember! You're here!*

Yes! Thank goodness! Where are you?

We found the caves, and we're looking for you. Do you know where you are?

Deception moved me to a large chamber with an opening that leads out to the seashore.

And is he there now?

No, no one is. He left with his men a few minutes ago to get some last things ready, but he could be back at any moment!

Then I'll be quick! Hold on! And Peace quickly turned and ran back toward the main chamber.

Most of the other men had already returned from their explorations by the time he got there. Justice was in discussion with one of them who was pointing excitedly down a passage. Peace didn't notice.

"Justice! I found him! He's this way."

Justice nodded to the man that he had been talking to then turned to face Peace. "You found Ember? Through the Link?"

"Yes! He's this way. We have to hurry—Deception is leaving with him any minute."

"Then we must be swift in getting the gate open. There is a passageway over here that leads directly into the keep. From there, we can make a break for the wall before anyone realizes what we're doing."

"What? We don't have time for that! We have to go for Ember now!"

"We need more men. As soon as we break through the gate—"

"Ember says that he's alone; if we go now, we won't need more men."

"Peace!" yelled Justice in frustration. "Can't you see this is a trap?"

Peace was surprised. "What you mean? I thought you said that we foiled Deception's trap when we found the tunnel."

"I said that *maybe* we did, but there's nothing that would stop him from having a second trap. Think about it. Ember can hear you which means he still has his Link. Why would Deception have allowed him to keep it? Why was this passage not guarded? He obviously *wants* you to find him."

Peace couldn't believe what his brother was saying. They were so close, and now it looked as though he would not help at all. "Maybe Deception didn't expect us to arrive yet. Ember said that he had left—"

"...Ember said? Why should we trust him?"

Peace's eyes darkened. "Are you really suggesting that Ember would betray us?"

"That would be a reasonable guess."

"Are you mad?" cried Peace. "Ember would never become a traitor! He would never want to hurt us! How can you possibly assume that—"

"All I know are the facts," said Justice. "One of which is that a man does not simply capture a dragon without a fight. There is a good chance that Ember could be working with Deception to trap both of us."

"You don't know him like I do; he would never do that—never in a thousand years!"

Justice shook his head and started down the tunnel that led to the keep. "Well, whether he would or not, it is obvious that you are walking into a trap and I have no intention of playing the fool any longer."

"Deception has never faced the wrath of a Rider deprived of his dragon. He underestimates who he's dealing with."

"You underestimate him! I know that you are determined, but I also know that Deception is cunning. He is prepared for whatever you might do."

"Then maybe that's the trap!" shot Peace. "Maybe he *wants* us to think he's prepared for us so that we *don't* attack him. What if he doesn't actually have a backup plan because he expects us to be overly cautious? What if this goes down as the day we let the greatest convict in history go without a fight because we were fooled by the simplest of tricks?"

"This is the peak of Deception's triumph. I doubt that he would now risk everything on a bluff."

"But you can't be sure."

Justice looked at him fiercely for moment, but then bowed his head. "No, I cannot be sure."

"Then I must go with what I am sure of—trap or not, Deception will leave with Ember and I must try to stop him. Please, brother; may I have your help in saving him?"

Justice looked at him firmly, but his eyes seemed to show a hint of hidden emotion. Then he said, "I cannot come with you. Everything about the idea seems rash and against sound judgment; I think that Deception is using your emotions against you, knowing how much you love your dragon."

Peace looked at him, crestfallen, as the men began to file down the other tunnel.

"However," said Justice, before turning to follow them, "knowing how much you love your dragon I would never try to stop *you* from going."

Peace looked back up at him and Justice smiled. "Hurry my brother! Stall them long enough and I'll be back to help as soon as I get the gate open. Good luck, and farewell." Then he turned and left.

Peace nodded, and then slowly turned his back and faced down his own tunnel—his path, his destiny. He drew his sword and held it high so that the flickering light of his lantern glimmered on its blade, and then he charged down into the darkness.

Perhaps there really was a trap or maybe Deception was just overconfident, but whatever the reason there were no guards along the tunnel as Peace ran. Soon he felt himself welcomed once again by Ember's consciousness and felt his excitement grow within him with every step that brought him closer.

Peace! You're coming! he heard his dragon say. *You were gone for so long, I wondered if you were going to come at all.*

No, I am here...though Justice is not. Are you still alone?

Yes; I can feel that you are very near me now. Watch yourself!

Peace looked up and saw that he was rushing for a great doorway at the end of the chamber. Two guards who stood at either side drew their swords as they saw him coming. But Peace was undaunted. He flashed his weapon in an arc and one of the guards fell to the ground. The other tried to swing his blade at him but Peace blocked and struck back before he had a chance to cry out, and then both soldiers were lying at his feet. He hardly noticed. With all his might, he pushed against the great doors and slowly they opened.

Peace suddenly found himself standing in a great room with pillars that towered up to the ceiling. At the far end stood Ember; each of his legs shackled to one of the great stone columns, but aside from that he was unbound. He shook his chains and bellowed in joy when he saw his Rider, and the light of the morning sun pouring in through a tall archway across the room seemed to make the dragon's scales glitter and shine in more vibrant emerald green than ever before. Peace gave a shout of joy himself and broke into a full-out sprint for his dragon, clearing the empty space of the chamber between them with blinding speed.

***

Deception crouched off to the side in the shadows behind Ember. Neither the Rider nor dragon could see him, and even as he stood and allowed the sunlight from the morning sun to fall upon his face, he knew that neither would notice for they were too focused on each other. He drew his saber and smiled wickedly as he watched Peace rushing toward the dragon with such joy. He had planned this so many times in his head, so many times he had dreamed of this moment, and at last it was...

Too quick! He noticed that Peace was moving very fast. More swiftly than he had expected. Deception felt a sickness grow in his stomach as he tried to judge how long it would be before the two met—and then he broke out into full sprint of his own. No! It could not end like this! He had come so far—he couldn't allow them to meet now! Peace was almost there, his hand outstretched to touch his precious dragon.

"No!" cried Deception leaping with all his might and landing hard between them—his left hand on the dragon's muzzle and his right pointing a sword at the Rider's throat.

Peace barely managed to bring himself to a halt without impaling himself on the blade. Under normal circumstances he would've knocked it aside with his own sword and kept running, but his mind was too startled with what was happening to Ember.

The dragon stood screeching and trembling beneath Deception's

hand. He rattled and yanked at his chains, but couldn't seem to pull himself away.

Through the Link, Peace heard traces of Ember's panicked thoughts, *Please stop! I can't...I can't...Help me! Peace!*

"Ember!" cried Peace, but he found now that his sword was lying on the ground and that his arms were being held tightly by two burly men.

Behind Deception, Ember struggled and fought, and Peace could sense flashes of feelings running through him. Feelings of pain, feelings of joy, feelings of deep sadness, of heartbreak, and of hunger. Feelings of a desperate thirst for something, a pleading thirst for something he could not name.

Ember slowly began to calm down—his struggles became less intense, his mind less troubled. Deception watched him wickedly, his one hand still pointing a sword at Peace's throat, but the other gently stroking the dragon scales. Then Ember relaxed completely, like a child lulled back to sleep after a nightmare. Peace tried to contact him, but he didn't seem to hear. All he got back was a steady stream of calm and content, like the purring of a cat in gentle hands.

"Ember!" cried Peace, struggling vainly against the guards. He turned to Deception. "What have you done to him?"

Deception chuckled. "What have I done? I've given him what he wanted—peace." He laughed wildly at his own joke.

Peace stared at him in horror, unable to understand. "Don't give me riddles!" he shouted. "Tell me what's wrong with him!"

Deception looked toward Ember longingly, and then turned back. "Allow me to explain something," he said. "You see, in all my years of exile I learned that no joy or happiness ever lasts forever. We enjoy the simplest things in life—eating, sleeping, admiring the beauty of a sunrise—but if you try to hold on to those feelings, to savor and enjoy them, they always disappear. We can't keep them, we can't control them. But what if..." and now Deception's eyes began to light up excitedly, "what if we could hijack our own souls? What if we could impart emotions to ourselves at will? How much would you give to have that ability? How much would any of us give to have infinite happiness apart from circumstances?"

Peace looked at him in bewilderment. "That would destroy us! Feelings of joy are meant to complement life, but they are not its final aim!"

"Oh, look who is telling lies now," snapped Deception. "Which of us doesn't spend every waking moment trying to become happier? Everything we do is centered on the pursuit of pleasure and the great irony is that, somehow, we can never achieve it.

"But look at Ember! Unlike us humans, he's already been broken. Thanks to you and Highland, his source of joy is not dependent on circumstances, but rather on us. Really, he is the blessed one here, for he alone is capable of feeling unending joy, continual pleasure, everlasting bliss...and as long as I touch him, I give it to him. Every moment he lives now he is living in absolute fulfillment.

"That is why he doesn't hear you; he doesn't need you anymore! Before, you were nothing more to him than a means to an end, though he probably never realized it. He stayed with you because you could bring him joy on occasion. There were plenty of times when if you touched him, and held a feeling of pure love for him in your mind, he would've reacted to you just as he reacted to me. But you didn't. You might've loved him, but he was also a means to your ends. He was your power source, and you needed him to maintain your control."

"I never saw him like that!" growled Peace in bitterness and rage. "He was my friend, my love; not my weapon!"

"Ah, but he was!" Deception said. He threw his head back and laughed at the ceiling. "You see! That was the beauty of the Dragon Rider Pact! That was what made you so unconquerable! The ultimate power source obeying a man of cunning and wisdom. But as soon as I step between you, what do you become? A pitiful human who can't match me in a sword fight, and a broken dragon desiring to be mastered by anyone. It took me nearly a decade in the wilderness to realize this principle."

Deception stroked Ember's neck. "But now I can finally use it to take what I've always wanted—a dragon of my own."

"Get your hands off of him!" cried Peace. "He's not your dragon!"

"Oh, he's not?" said Deception, smiling wickedly. "Because I think he rather prefers me."

He reached around Ember's neck and gently removed the Link. Tossing it to the ground, he pulled out another chain with a medallion on it and slipped it over Ember's horns in the Link's place.

"He is mine now. He will fly wherever I want him to fly, he will do as I tell him to do. He will even let me kill him if I want. I am his new master, and no one will ever take him from me."

Several more guards approached and began to unchain the dragon from the pillars. Ember didn't even seem to notice. He continued to stare contentedly at Deception.

"No!" cried Peace, throwing off one of the guards with a burst of strength and lunging toward him. Soldiers quickly grabbed him and pulled him back. "You can't take him!" he yelled. "I will never allow it! Highland will find you! You will not get away with this!"

"Oh, but I will!" said Deception, smiling again. Peace hated that grin. "I will fly with him off to another land, the Shadowlands, which is beyond the King's domain. I hid there myself all these years, avoiding detection. Nearly all of my men have already sailed there. The last ship left less than an hour ago and soon we, me and my dragon, shall follow them."

"Do you think the King is contained by seas? He will find you! You will not escape!"

"But tell me, how will the King have time to search for me when his own kingdom is falling apart?"

"What do you mean by that?"

Deception shook his head disapprovingly. "My dear boy, don't you see? Too many kingdoms have sat under the rule of Highland for too long. They flocked willingly to me when I promised to rid them of the Dragon Rider. Now that I have, six of the greatest kingdoms shall rise up together and attack Highland as soon as I am gone. And while your King is busy protecting himself, I will rally my own army in the Shadowlands and strike with a force so large that none will be able to stand before me! Your father, and his kingdom, will be destroyed!"

Deception leaned forward and whispered in Peace's ear, "I even have dragons in the Shadowlands."

He saw the surprise in Peace's face and laughed. "Yes," he said. "Ember is not my first dragon. I never would've attempted this conquest had I not successfully completed the process on many before. But he will be different than the others. He will be my personal dragon, for he was part of the Dragon Rider Pact. In a way, he is even heir to the throne...which makes his *Rider* heir to the throne as well, doesn't it? How fitting will it be when I come back with my armies and conquer Highland—my inheritance?"

Deception walked up to Ember and mounted him. "In a way, I really have you to thank for this," he said to Peace. "You raised him, and for three years you prepared him for me to ride. You've had your time and now it's my turn. I thank you for your generous gift...your grandfather never saw fit to give one to me."

"Please!" begged Peace, struggling weakly against the guards. "Take me instead. Kill me if you want, but please don't take him!"

Deception stared at Peace with an odd look in his eyes as he considered the request. Then he dismounted and walked toward him. He picked up Peace's own sword from the ground. "You know," he said. "I really do want to kill you."

He held the blade against Peace's throat. "I've thought about it so many times. So many years I went through this in my head, and I always looked forward to killing you."

He drew back the blade and held it high to strike.

"It seemed so perfect—kill the Rider and take his dragon. It was going to be my revenge." And then suddenly he smiled, and his eyes grew wicked. "But then I thought of something better."

He threw Peace's sword to the ground, where it clattered next to Ember's Link. "You see," Deception said, walking back toward Ember who stood waiting for him silently, "killing you would be too quick. I didn't want to just conquer you—I wanted to see you suffer!"

He mounted the dragon and held his saber high. "You would give your life for your dragon if you thought that you could save him, and if he were murdered you would kill yourself rather than live without him. But instead, I'm going to keep him alive and just out of your reach. You can't bear death as long as there's the possibility of saving him, and you can't bear life knowing he's in my hands. It will be absolute agony for you! I want you alive; I want you watching helplessly as I fly your dragon off across the sea beyond your reach. This is my victory—my victory at World's End!"

He laughed wildly and turned Ember toward the great archway that led to the seashore. "Maybe I'll kill you when I return to claim Highland," he said without turning back. "You'll be nothing more than another person running around down there anyway."

And then he rode Ember out through the archway, turned around the corner, and traveled up the seashore out of view.

Peace shrieked and threw himself against the guards, struggling to get out of their grasp. They held his arms firmly, but he struggled hard, a power he did not know rushing through him. And then the soldier gripping his right arm cried out and fell to the ground with a dagger in his back. Peace looked behind him.

"Justice!" he cried. His brother was galloping toward him on a horse, his katana held high. Peace felt around on the ground for his sword and struck at the other guard while he was still distracted. He fell to the ground along with the first and Peace stood free.

"Hurry!" cried Justice leaping off his horse which continued to gallop straight ahead toward Peace. "Stop Deception! He's heading down the shore; maybe you can catch him!"

Peace scooped up Ember's Link from the floor and swung himself into the saddle as the horse charged by. Looking behind, he saw Justice fighting with two of the guards as ten more closed in. The soldiers of Highland however were pouring in from the doorway.

"Just go!" yelled Justice, his sword swinging with lightning speed. "Stop him!"

Peace turned back and shielded his eyes as he rode through the archway toward the glittering sea. Then he turned to follow in the same direction that Deception had gone.

He galloped down the sand for several minutes with the mountains on his left and the sea on his right. The sun, which before had only just begun to peek up over the watery horizon, now bloomed into a brilliant half circle of fire and light which cascaded across the gentle waves of the sea.

Peace came upon them as he rounded a bend. Ember stood, with Deception beside him, looking out over the sea at a ship sailing away on the horizon. Peace rode to about a stone's throw away and then dismounted. The two did not seem to notice his presence, so he slowly and cautiously began to advance toward them.

Then, without turning his head from the sunrise, Deception addressed him, "Do you really hope to change anything?"

Peace did not answer. His hand was on his sword hilt, but he did not draw it; not yet. He kept trying to approach Ember.

But then, there was Deception, blocking his way. "Peace, please," he said. "I really don't want to kill you here." He drew his saber.

"Give me back Ember, and I will let you go."

"Let me go?" laughed Deception. "This is my victory! That ship out there has the last of my men, and soon I shall follow them. Why should I give up everything now?"

"Not many are offered mercy like this," said Peace coldly. "I won't offer it to you again."

"Then I refuse! What do you say to that? Let's see what you do when diplomacy fails."

Peace unleashed his fury. With lightning speed, he drew his sword and swung at Deception's saber, knocking him aside. Then he leapt toward Ember, who was just turning to see what had happened.

"No!" cried Deception rushing after him, but Peace was faster, and before he could be stopped, he leapt forth and placed his hand on Ember's forehead.

Instantly a struggle followed inside the dragon and Peace felt it all through his Link. At first, he only felt a sudden surge of pain and guilt...and then he felt it—a determination within Ember that fought against the pleasure which held him captive! He felt a fragment of consciousness emerge that was still Ember, still the dragon he knew. He felt it leap forth from the confusion of his mind and try to reach him.

And then it was slain. The fragment of consciousness was snuffed out like a rebel shot as he comes out of hiding, like a spark touching a cold floor. Like a dying ember.

With shock and despair Peace tried again to reach him, but this time he was met only with the mind of Deception's dragon—a dragon furious at him. He turned in horror back to Deception who stood smiling.

"Did you really think I would leave my dragon without a safeguard?" he asked. Beneath Peace's hand, Ember growled threateningly. Deception laughed in triumph. "He's cursed now. Never again will he serve anyone except for me."

Peace stared at his dragon in disbelief. His left hand gently stroked the scales of his lost friend...and then his right hand tightened around his sword! With a cry he swung around at Deception, striking his saber. The blow knocked Deception backwards and Peace kept after him, hacking wildly and relentlessly until he managed to knock the weapon out of his opponent's hand. His adversary fell to the ground and held up his arm as if to ward off the blow as Peace raised his sword above his head.

And flame engulfed it. With a cry, Peace dropped his sword and clutched his burned hand.

Deception took his chance and grabbing his saber hit Peace hard on the head with the hilt, knocking him down. He ran toward his dragon, which stood crouched and ready to blast fire again, mounted, and turned it away from its former master toward the sea.

Peace tried desperately to get up as the world spun around him. He saw Ember running toward the seashore with Deception on his back, and with a cry he blindly grabbed his sword with his left hand and chased after them. But the dragon spread its wings and leaped into the sky, leaving him behind.

***

And so the Dragon Rider stood abandoned on the shore of a glittering sea, a scorched sword hanging limply from his hand, as he watched the vanishing form of a ship sailing calmly into the sunrise—and above it, the silhouette of a man on his dragon, leading it in triumph toward a distant land. Such was the outcome of the battle at World's End.

End of Part One